TAKEN BY THE DRAGON

JESSICA GRAYSON
ARIA WINTER

Copyright @ 2020 by Jessica Grayson & Aria Winter

Taken By The Dragon All rights reserved under International and Pan American Copyright Conventions.

By payment of the required fees, you have been granted the nonexclusive, nontransferable right to access and read the text of this e-book on-screen.

No part of this text may be reproduced, transmitted, downloaded, decompiled, reverse-engineered, or stored in or introduced into any information storage and retrieval system, in any form or by any means, whether electronic or mechanical, now known or hereafter invented, without the written permission of Jessica Grayson & Aria Winter except for the use of brief quotations in a book review.

This is a work of fiction. Names, characters, businesses, places, events and incidents are either the products of the author's imagination or used in a fictitious manner. Any resemblance to actual persons, living or dead, or actual events is purely coincidental.

Published in the United States by Purple Fall Publishing. Purple Fall Publishing and the Purple Fall Publishing Logos are trademarks and/or registered trademarks of Purple Fall Publishing LLC.

Publisher's Cataloging-in-Publication data

Names: Grayson, Jessica, author. | Winter, Aria, author.

Title: Taken by the dragon : a Beauty and the Beast retelling / Jessica Grayson & Aria Winter

Series: Once Upon a Fairy Tale Romance

Description: Purple Fall Publishing, 2020.

Identifiers: ISBN:

978-1-64253-413-9 (ebook)

978-1-64253-315-6 (pbk.)

978-1-64253-303-3 (audio)

Subjects: LCSH Dragons--Fiction. | Shapeshifting--Fiction. | Love stories. | Romance fiction. | Fantasy fiction. | BISAC FICTION / Romance / Fantasy | FICTION / Fantasy / Romantic | FICTION / Fantasy / Dragons & Mythical Creatures | FICTION / Fairy Tales, Folk Tales, Legends & Mythology

Classification: PS3623 .I6675 T35 2020 | DDC 813.6--dc23

Cover Design by Kim Cunningham of Atlantis Book Design

PRINTED IN THE UNITED STATES OF AMERICA

DEDICATION

To my husband: You are not just my husband, you are my best friend and my rock. Thank you for all your love and support. I love you more than words can ever say.

-Jessica Grayson

CHAPTER 1

ALARA

I cannot see the blood moon that shines overhead this night, but I can feel the fear that it brings. The muffled sounds of my sister crying in the arms of her beloved next door fill me with sadness.

She is to be sacrificed to the Dragon tomorrow. The terrifying beast that lives in the castle by the sea. My best friend, Mara, was chosen last year. None have ever returned.

For as long as I can remember, it has always been this way. Each year, when the blood moon rises, a maiden is chosen from the village. She is taken to the edge of the forest where, bound and blindfolded, she is left as an offering to the beast.

Cursed by a blood witch, legend says he is both monster and man. Able to walk the earth in a human form beneath the red moon, none may look upon his two-legged form during this time without turning to stone.

The King of Eryadon sent his best knights to slay the beast, but their weapons could not even pierce its thick scales. It is now said that no weapon created by man can slay a Dragon.

That is why we must appease him each year with a maiden.

All know that the sacrifice is necessary, but that does not make it any easier to accept.

I can hardly bear the thought of my sister's fate. She is everything to me, and I cannot image a life without her.

I slip from my bed and creep into the hallway. Quietly, I place my ear to her door.

"I won't let you go," Garen says, his voice thick with emotion. "I'll kill the beast before I'll let it take you."

"You can't," Lilly whimpers. "He'll kill you. And I don't want you to die, my love. Only one of us has to die, not both."

I squeeze my eyes shut against the pain. Not that I can see anything, but it helps to hold in my tears. The plague that claimed our mother and father eight years ago is the same one that took my vision.

"I cannot bear it." Garen's voice quavers. "I don't want to lose you. I want our future together, Lilly."

I place my open palm to the door as I hang my head and swallow back a sob. I cannot lose my sister. Not Lilly.

She has watched over me ever since our parents died. My older sister will be twenty-five in a few months. She has a kind and handsome fiancé and—if not for the Dragon—a beautiful future awaiting her with long years full of children and grandchildren.

Whereas I have nothing but her.

Lilly doesn't have to be the sacrifice. I will go in her stead.

Resolved to my fate, I bow my head and send a silent prayer to the gods and our parents to watch over Lilly and Garen. *Please, give them a long and happy life,* I pray.

And please, let me be brave.

CHAPTER 2

ALARA

The warmth of the sun as it filters in through my window awakens me. I did not sleep well last night. It was impossible to ignore my sister's tears as she cried in Garen's arms. He promised her he would care for me for the rest of my life. He is an honest man and has been our friend since childhood. I know he will be a good husband to her.

With a heavy sigh, I get up from the bed. I do not bother to pack any of my belongings. After all, I do not know how long the Dragon will let me live.

Although I can no longer see, I remember how to write. I know every room in this house by heart, and it doesn't take long to find paper and quill. I scribble a farewell as best I can, fold the paper, and leave it on the kitchen table. By the time my sister and Garen find it, I will already be gone.

I grab my walking cane to guide me, stopping just outside the front door to rest my hand on the garden wall. "Goodbye, Lilly," I whisper.

It's colder now that winter is upon us, and I wrap my shawl tightly around my shoulders against the chill. The ground is soft from the fresh snow that fell last night, making walking a bit more difficult than normal as I navigate the unfamiliar path to the edge of the forest.

I've only been here one other time. I accompanied Mara when she was chosen last year. We said a tearful goodbye, and then she told me to leave and made me promise to never return.

Today, I am breaking my vow, but I believe she would not hold it against me if she knew my reasons.

The smell of damp earth and vegetation surrounds me, and I know I am getting closer as the forest becomes still and silent. It is as if all the woodland creatures know what is coming this day.

Steadily, I make my way up the small hill. Someone clears their throat up ahead and I stop.

"Alara, what are you doing here?"

I recognize the mayor's voice and do my best to keep my expression neutral. I don't want him to see me afraid because I know whatever he sees now, he will undoubtedly report to my sister and the rest of the town. I want her to believe I faced my fate with little fear. "I'm here to take the place of Lilly."

He's silent. In truth, I did not expect him to protest, but it hurts just the same. I am the more logical choice for a sacrifice because of my blindness. One thing about losing my vision is that all my other senses became heightened in compensation.

I'm sure many of the townspeople do not realize this, for I often hear them whispering when I go to the market with my sister. They pity me but feel even worse for Lilly because they believe I am such a tremendous burden to her.

That's one of many reasons I've tried to become as independent as possible. With my walking cane, I can navigate most any path without aid. I am able to tell one coin from another by its size and the weight in my palm. But when people look at me, all they see is a broken thing. A girl who used to be whole but is now only a burden to her family.

Well, after today, they will not have to feel sorry for me any longer. I have never wanted their pity, anyway.

The mayor clears his throat again. The thick slush of snow and mud muffles the sound of his boots as he approaches. A subtle sucking noise joins each step, growing louder until he is standing beside me. "You are still a maiden, are you not?" he asks meekly.

Unable to speak around the knot in my throat, I nod. Of course, I am. I am twenty-three years old. The king forbids every woman to marry or know the touch of a man until the age of twenty-five. For it is known that the beast only accepts maidens as his sacrifice.

When I lost my vision, I gained the ability to visualize colors that signify people's state of mind. Today, the mayor's color is gray, though most days he is blue. Gray is the shade of sadness and it helps me to know that, even if he does not protest my self-sacrifice, at least he cares in a way.

A bright and beautiful pink aura of joy always surrounds my sister, whereas Garen's constant worrying tints him a variation of orange. More often lately, as their wedding day approaches, he is pink as well, his happiness matching that of my sister's.

A warm hand takes mine. "I'll lead you the rest of the way," the mayor says.

He walks slowly for my sake, I'm sure. Although his voice is calm as he tells me how this all works, his callused palm is damp with perspiration. His color changes to a darker orange and I cannot tell if his worry is for me or for himself.

It could be either, or both, for it is his job to stand blindfolded nearby when the Dragon comes, to make sure that everything goes according to plan. It would not do to leave a maiden unsupervised only for her to run off, denying the beast his sacrifice and damning the kingdom to destruction and ruin.

He takes my walking cane and guides first my left hand, and then my right to the two poles where I'll be tied while waiting for the beast to retrieve me. Even though I'm here of my own volition, he binds my wrists rather tightly, probably worried I might have second thoughts.

"I guess I won't need to blindfold you," he mutters, and I realize he is speaking more to himself than to me.

Right now, it is all I can do to keep what I hope is an impassive expression on my face, so I say nothing.

"All right then," he says. "It's almost time." His footsteps begin to retreat before he pauses, adding, "Thank you for your sacrifice. Do you have any last words for your sister?"

"Tell her…" My bottom lip quivers, and I swallow against the lump in my throat. "Please, tell her I was unafraid and that I love her."

"I will," he assures me, his steps growing distant. I hear him stop before he blows the horn. The deep, reverberating sound echoes through the woods, sending a chill down my spine.

I know it well—everyone does. This horn calls the Dragon to collect his sacrifice—the chosen maiden from the village.

Today, *I* am the sacrifice.

My heart hammers as time seems to crawl. The forest is eerily still, growing more hushed by the second, as if every living creature is as tense as I am, waiting for the death that is to come.

I whisper under my breath to the gods and to my parents,

whom I believe are watching over me. "Please," I pray. "Let me be brave."

A deafening roar splits the air. The Dragon is here. He is coming to take me.

CHAPTER 3

ALARA

Another bellowing roar sounds as the great flapping of wings fills my ears. Strong wind gusts around me, tearing at my dress. I close my eyes against the dust and debris. The ground trembles beneath my feet and a warm puff of air parts the hair on the top of my head.

"Do not open your eyes," a deep voice rumbles from above me. "If you view me in this form, you will instantly turn to stone."

A disturbing thought I had not considered before enters my mind. What if he rejects me as the sacrifice because of my blindness? I squeeze my eyes tightly shut so he will not know.

The whipping wind settles to a cool breeze, and the smell of fresh rain and forest fills my nostrils. I breathe deeply of the wonderful scent. Is this the Dragon I smell?

"Hold still." His voice is smooth and deep with a rough edge, the words thick as if trying to form around too many teeth.

Dragons are cold, calculating, and vicious predators. Fear skitters up my spine. I have never been so close to one before.

About a year after I lost my sight, I decided I would stop lamenting its absence. Missing something that you cannot have back is consuming, and I realized I had to let it go. However, as the Dragon stands before me, I wish for the first time since then that I could still see. I would like to know exactly what is coming for me and how he will exact my death.

Something tugs at my dress, and I gasp at the sound of ripping fabric.

"What are you doing?" The mayor's voice rings out.

Soft material touches my face as he ties a strip around my head. "You did not blindfold her as instructed," the Dragon grinds out. "I should kill you for this level of neglect."

The coloring surrounding him is solid red with anger, sparking fear in my heart. Not just for my safety, but also the mayor's.

Panic coils tight in my chest. Is the mayor going to give away my secret? Explain to the Dragon I am blind?

I hold my breath, waiting for the mayor to speak, but he says nothing aside from a hastily mumbled apology. So, even *he* knows better than to tell the Dragon of my disability. At least we agree in this regard.

Then again, what does it matter anyway? I am the sacrifice. I do not expect to live long enough for the Dragon to find out.

A large hand curls around my forearm. It's warm against my skin, but not uncomfortably so. He rips the binding from one wrist and my hand drops freely to my side. He takes my other wrist and frees that hand as well.

Despite my attempt to appear unfazed, my entire body is trembling, and I can barely hear anything over the pounding of my pulse in my ears as I wait for what he will do next.

"I am going to shift into my Dragon form and carry you now."

I wonder why he's even bothering to warn me. Why tell me about his plans? I'm the sacrifice. He can do with me as he wishes. Even as I ponder this, his color changes to light red—the color of agitation.

I'm so terrified I cannot speak, so I do my best to nod and say nothing. He's already irritated, and I do not want to anger him further.

A frigid blast of air whips around me, then an enormous hand circles my torso, lifting me off the ground. I reach out and touch something hard, yet sleek as silk. If these are scales, they do not feel as rough as I imagined they would. I continue tracing my fingers over his flesh until I reach something smooth like glass. It tapers to a fine point, and I swallow nervously when I realize it is a talon at least the length of my forearm.

His grip tightens before dust and cold wind whirl around us as he lifts into the air. At first, our flight is turbulent, his entire body shuddering as the wind rips at our forms. He dips to one side, and the air suddenly calms, as if we are no longer fighting the current.

His deep voice sounds. "When we arrive at the castle, you must keep your blindfold on, or you will turn to stone. Do you understand?"

I'm nauseated from the initial rough start to our flight, and I fear that I'll violently expel the contents of my stomach. The slight up and down motion as we glide through the air reminds me of the last time I was on a ship in the harbor, weathering the gentle waves. I've been afraid of heights since I was a child, but since I cannot see, I can easily imagine that I'm floating on the water instead of flying high above the ground. It helps calm my pounding heart as we continue our journey to his castle.

"Yes," I finally respond.

Despite all of this, I am far from all right, but what does it matter? I'm not long for this world, anyway. Better to just keep quiet and get this over with as quickly as possible. I don't know in what gruesome way the Dragon plans to dispose of me; I only know that I'd rather not suffer any longer than I must.

After an eternity, his body begins to sway back and forth. My long hair whips around my face with the heavy beat of his wings. Just as I'm about to ask what's going on, we settle with a *thud*.

Carefully, his talons unwrap from my body, and I begin to slide from his palm. Fear fills me at the prospect of falling. Dragons are known to make their homes high in the mountains, and this one supposedly lives in an abandoned and ancient castle on the cliffs by the sea.

That is why no one ventures into the forest between the village and the ocean. No one has ever verified this, however, and we could be anywhere, for all I know. My mind conjures an image of a cliff, and I cling to him, afraid to let go and tumble to my death.

A blast of icy air whips around me, and suddenly, two strong hands encircle my waist. The shift is so unexpected, I let out a small squeak of surprise.

My feet touch the ground and I release the breath I hadn't realized I was holding. "Thank you," I whisper.

His hands fall away from my body, leaving me alone. Without my walking cane, I feel helpless in a way I have not since the early days when I first lost my sight.

I push down my anxiety as I focus on using all my remaining senses. A familiar sound draws my attention and my head snaps in its direction. The dull roar of waves crashing along the shoreline carries on a crisp, saline breeze. "Are we near the ocean?"

"Yes. My castle sits on a cliff wall above the sea."

Cliff. The rumors are true. My fear of falling is not entirely unfounded, it seems.

I freeze, afraid to take one wrong step and tumble to my death. I may be about to die, and one death is probably just as bad as another, but I don't want to risk falling and breaking my back or my legs and suffering in such a state until I starve or die of infection.

Shakily, I extend my arm in the direction I last heard his voice. "Where—where are you?"

A warm hand takes mine, his palm smooth against my skin. It is much larger than any hand I've ever held before, and I have held many. Especially in the early days of my blindness.

"Come," he says. "I will show you to your room."

"My room?"

"Yes."

My chest constricts painfully. Is he taking me to the room where he means to kill me? I do not regret taking my sister's place, but even so, I'm not ready to die just yet. I stop abruptly, tugging on his arm to buy myself some time. "Wait."

"What is it?" he asks, his voice gruff and his color shifting to silver.

I've never sensed silver on anyone in the past, and I wonder what it means. The colorful auras have always helped me to determine a person's nature and whether they mean me harm. His consistent silver coloring prevents me from discerning his mood or intentions.

"I'm Alara," I speak softly. "What is your name?"

"I am known as the Dragon. Or Beast."

I shake my head slightly. "But those are not names. If you walk in the form of a man, surely you have a name."

He is silent for so long, I wonder if he is even going to reply. I swallow nervously, trying to think of some other way to draw him out and delay my impending doom.

"My name is Veron," he finally answers.

"Veron," I repeat aloud. *A good, strong name*, my mother would have said.

Perhaps it's my lack of sight that makes me brave, but I want to at least know more about this man who is going to take my life. Maybe I can convince him to take pity on me and let me live instead.

"May I touch you?"

He goes quiet and still, his silver color shifting again to an angry red. After a long pause, he replies, "If you think to seduce me to win your freedom, it will not work. The curse prevents me from releasing you. If you are gone from this place for more than a day, I will turn into a mindless and destructive beast, intent upon finding you. I will raze your village to the ground and several towns beyond that in my search."

I can't breathe, for now I realize that I have no chance. I cannot leave and risk him harming others because I am gone. Now, I understand why no one has ever returned from this place before. Soon, I will die.

It would be easy to give in to despair, but if I've learned anything after losing my sight, it is that hope should never be easily tossed away. "What must be done to break the curse?"

"It cannot be done," he says, irritation evident in his voice. "If it could, I would have broken the curse long ago. Unless…" He trails off.

I will not be deterred. If there is a chance that I may live to see my sister again, I must try. "What is it? Tell me."

"You must look upon me in my two-legged form and recognize me as your true love." His color shifts between the strange silver and light red. "But that can never happen, for all who view me in this form, during the blood moon cycle, will turn to stone."

"But how would anyone break the curse then?" I ask incredulously. "It does not make sense."

"Indeed," he replies bitterly. "The one who cursed me was as cruel as she is clever."

I swallow back my disappointment. Without my sight, I cannot lay eyes upon him at all. I do not tell him this, however, because the truth will do neither of us any good. I consider his words and ask just to be certain. "I have one lunar cycle before I will die?"

He hesitates so long in answering, all I can hear is the hammering of my heart in my chest. "Yes," he murmurs. "It is part of the curse."

"How will it happen?" I must know. "How will I die?"

"You will fade away and simply cease to be."

He says the words with such an air of finality, it forms a hollow ache in my chest. I will fade away as if I had never existed.

I lower my head and swallow against the lump in my throat. In this moment, I have accepted my fate. It is not every day that one learns the date and manner of one's death. Now that I know, I would like to live what little time I have left to the best of my ability, and I must try to live it without fear. I send a silent prayer to the gods. *Please. Let me be brave.*

"I'd still like to touch you. May I?"

"Why would you wish to do this?" His tone is hard and wary. "If you think to trick me or harm me, know that your kind are no match for a Dragon."

I gesture to my blindfold. "It is the only way I will know what you look like. And I am curious to know to whom I am speaking."

"I am a beast," he growls. "Do you truly wish to touch a monster?"

"You are not a monster," I reply as evenly as I can despite my fear. "You are Veron, and you are the person with whom I will spend my final days. So, yes," I state firmly, trying to appear brave, "I would like to touch you and learn who you are. If you will allow me to."

"Fine."

Drawing in a deep and steeling breath, I step closer to him. So close that the heat from his body radiates to mine. His masculine scent surrounds me, so thick I can almost taste the fresh rain and the forest on my tongue.

I reach out and somehow find his hand. I do not know if he extended it to me or not. I trace my fingers over his palm, marveling at the silken texture of his flesh.

"Do you have scales?" The question escapes my lips before I even realize I've spoken it aloud.

"Yes. Why?"

"I was just... wondering. They feel so smooth, I was not sure."

He falls silent again, so I continue my exploration.

He has five fingers tipped with dagger-sharp claws. As I probe his fingertips, I feel them retract. My hands trail up his arms, my fingers brushing over thick cords of muscle. His shoulders are broad and strong. He's so tall, the top of my head sits just below his chin. I stretch up on my toes to reach him better when I feel him bend down a bit. That's rather considerate, I think to myself.

He certainly feels like a regular man—in shape, anyway. This helps calm some of my fear.

With slightly ridged brows, an aristocratic nose, and a strong, square jaw, I imagine he must be very handsome. I gently feel along his full, warm lips, trying to visualize his face in my mind.

A thought occurs to me. "What color is your skin? I mean... your scales," I correct.

"Silver."

I nod, trying to picture an attractive man with silver scales.

"What about your eyes?"

"Dark green. The color of emeralds."

A smile tugs at my lips. Of course, a Dragon would compare his eyes to a precious jewel. Everyone knows they covet gems and treasure.

I move down his neck to his chest. My fingers glide over thick planes of muscle. As I travel down to his abdomen, I realize not an ounce of fat lies beneath his scales.

He grabs my wrists abruptly with one hand, halting my exploration of his body. "Stop." A low and menacing growl rumbles deep in his chest.

My veins fill with ice. "I—I'm sorry," I barely manage, as he frees my trembling arms. "Did I do something wrong?"

"I may be a Dragon, but I am also a male."

My brow furrows in confusion until realization dawns. My touch excited him like it would any man. Heat scalds my cheeks. "I—I'm sorry. I did not mean to—"

I freeze. He could do anything he wants to me. I am his prisoner… the sacrifice given to appease him. Dread skitters up my spine as I wonder what exactly that may entail.

His color shifts between red and that strange silver again. He huffs out a breath. "You stink of fear, human. Do not worry, I would not touch you in that way." A hint of disgust laces his tone. "My kind do not mate with yours."

"It's Alara," I correct.

"What?" he asks, obviously irritated.

"My *name* is Alara."

Silence stretches between us before he finally mutters, "Your name does not matter."

My mouth drifts open at his rudeness. "It matters to *me*," I snap, furious at being dismissed in such a way. "And if we're going to be together—"

"We will *not* be together," he snarls. "I already told you—my kind do not mate yours. My body responded to you because you are the first person to touch me in many years. That is all."

Though I probably should be offended, I pity him in a way. Touch is everything to me. Without it, I would be lost in the dark. Even when I had my sight, I valued that sense the most. My mind drifts back to long summer days, walking arm in arm with my sister through lavender fields.

Instead of telling him all this, however, I simply explain, "I don't mean that we would be mating. All I meant was that we will be spending time together."

He falls silent again and I wish so much that I could see because the silver color of his aura tells me absolutely nothing about his emotional state. "Come," he finally says, taking my hand. "I will take you to your room."

"All right."

The soft crunching of gravel beneath our feet gives way to the sharp slap of solid stone. Following the heavy creak of a door opening on old hinges, our footsteps echo hollowly. This space must be very large, and I wonder what it looks like.

"You said you live in a castle?"

"Yes."

"Could you describe it to me?"

He stops abruptly, hesitating for so long, I wonder if he will answer.

"Well?" I press, my tone one of gentle yet firm encouragement. I would like to be able to imagine the space that I'm in. Wouldn't anyone feel the same?

"It is… large."

I wait for him to continue. When he does not, I ask, "Any details you could share?"

He clears his throat as if unsure how to proceed. After another long moment of silence, he speaks. "The entire structure is built of gray stone. Four towers with silver capped domes mark the corners. The main entrance we just passed lies beneath an even larger dome, which sits directly in the middle of the castle."

"Any decorations?"

"Tapestries depicting glorious battles drape the walls. In the corner is a large stone fireplace stacked high with thick cords of wood. On the opposite wall, a row of floor-to-ceiling windows overlooks the sea."

"I imagine this place must be beautiful," I murmur, more to myself than to him.

"Is that good enough?" he asks gruffly.

"For now," I reply. "You'll have to be my eyes while I'm here and—"

"I am a Dragon, not a servant," he rumbles. "I will leave so you may remove your blindfold and see for yourself. Your room is up the stairs, the last door on the left at the end of the hall. And whatever you do, do not venture into the west wing."

"Why?"

"It is forbidden," he snarls, reminding me he is a Dragon, not a man. "I will alert you of my return so you may cover your eyes."

He relinquishes his grip on my hand and his footsteps retreat.

"Veron?" I call out, but he does not pause, nor does he answer.

The loud creak of the front door opening echoes throughout the space and then the door slams shut.

My heart begins hammering wildly. I'm alone in the dark.

And although I have been this way since I lost my sight, this is the first time in many years that I've been afraid. Shakily, I extend my hand, searching for any type of surface to guide me.

Now that my walking cane is gone, I realize just how much confidence it gives me and I wish I'd found a way to bring it here instead of leaving it behind. With my arms outstretched, I cautiously shuffle forward, trying to find a wall or a piece of furniture—anything that will give me some sense of where I am and what else is in this room.

I need to find the stairs, but I also need to avoid the west wing, wherever that is. My breath comes in short, clipped pants as I recall how adamant he was about me staying out of there.

My entire body trembles as my mind conjures all sorts of horrors that could await me in that part of the castle. Panic threatens to overwhelm me, but I have to focus. I need to find the stairs.

Breathing in and out through pursed lips, I concentrate on exploring my surroundings. I sigh with relief when I find a banister. Tracing my fingers along the surface, I detect intricately carved designs of swirling vines and leaves engraved in the wood. It must be beautiful, and I cannot imagine the long hours involved in making such a thing.

Cautiously, I begin to ascend, counting each step as I go. I'm only on number thirteen when a thunderous roar splits the air, startling me abruptly. Alarmed, I lose my grip on the handrail, shrieking as I fall back and tumble down the stairs.

My arms and legs flail wildly a moment as I desperately try to grab onto something to halt my descent before I tuck myself into a ball, tensing at every jarring bump along the way down.

When I finally stop, my head is spinning so badly I can

barely lift it. I draw in a shaking breath. Everything hurts and I'm afraid to move, worried I may have broken something.

Warm liquid trails down my forehead and drips onto my cheek. The metallic scent of iron fills my nostrils. I reach up to touch my scalp, gritting my teeth in pain as my fingers trace across a small laceration. I carefully sit up and shove my hair out of my face, smearing something warm and wet that I'm certain is blood through the long, blonde strands.

My blindfold is missing. I sweep my hands along the floor to search for it, but find nothing. Loud footsteps approach and I still as dread pools in my stomach.

"Shut your eyes!" Veron thunders, and then I hear him run toward me.

Flinching, I lift my arms out before me and brace to shield myself from his wrath.

He stops as soon as he reaches me. Something touches my face and I jerk away, hitting the back of my head on a hard surface that I assume is the wall. "Stay still!" he commands.

I try to do what he says, but I am trembling uncontrollably as his aura color shifts between red and silver. "Were you intentionally trying to kill yourself?"

"No, I—"

"Did you think to end your life to escape me?" he growls. "Foolish human."

"I wasn't trying to kill myself." My voice quavers slightly. "I swear."

"Then, what happened?"

"I was on the staircase when you... roared and it startled me, causing me to fall."

He huffs out a frustrated breath. "You need to be more careful."

"Why do you care?" I snap and then quickly clamp a hand over my mouth, surprised at the harshness of my tone.

A low growl rumbles deep in his chest. "Because while you are here, you are my responsibility."

"What does that mean?"

Instead of answering, I feel him wrap the blindfold back around my head to cover my eyes.

"Can you stand?"

"I…" I hesitate a moment as I test my limbs. Sharp pain shoots through my left wrist as I flex it and I inhale sharply.

"What's wrong?"

"My wrist. It hurts." I hiss as I test it again, satisfied when I don't hear any sort of cracking noise. I may not be a healer, but my mother was. She taught us as much as she could, and I am able to tell the difference between a break and a sprain. "I think it's just sprained."

He grips my forearm and pulls it toward him. Warm air puffs against my skin. "Why are humans such fragile creatures?" he mutters. "I suppose I'll have to heal you."

Offended by his condescending statement, I jerk my arm from his grasp. "I don't need your help. It will heal on its own."

He growls and grabs my forearm firmly. "Be still," he commands.

I freeze as my fear gets the best of me. His color shifts from silver to red and I worry I've pushed him too far.

Still holding my arm with one hand, he grips my palm with the other. His hands are now on either side of my injured wrist. Warmth spreads from the contact of his scales upon my skin, traveling to the site of my injury. Like a soothing balm, the heat spreads through my wrist and I sag forward in relief as the pain slowly fades and then disappears completely.

He lets go and I bend my wrist, turning it this way and that as I test it. A smile curves my lips. There is not even the slightest hint of discomfort.

He moves his hands up to the cut on my head and the same warmth spreads as the blood stops dripping.

"They're healed," I murmur in disbelief. "I did not realize Dragons could do such a thing." I reach for him, placing my hand over his when I find it and squeeze it gently. "Thank you, Veron."

"Try not to hurt yourself again," he grumbles. "Do you think you can manage that while you are here?"

The scorn in his tone makes me bristle slightly. His aura color is a lighter red now, indicating he is merely irritated instead of angry. And the fact that he just healed me means he does *not* want to hurt me. "Yes."

"Good. Now, I will take you to your room."

We ascend the flight of stairs. I appreciate how carefully he guides my every step. When we reach the top of the staircase, he describes a long corridor lined with tapestries and paintings. I do my best to listen and count at the same time. If this is to be my home for the month, I need to be able to find my way around by myself. I cannot expect him to guide me everywhere. He has already expressed that he does not wish to do this, anyway.

We stop, and I hear the latch of the door as he opens it. "This will be your room while you are here. Do not forget your blindfold anytime you step outside of these chambers."

My brow furrows. I remember him saying my room was down the hall on the left, but we made no left turn. "I thought you said my room would be on the left side of the hallway?"

"Do you want this room or not?"

I stand there a moment, uncertain how to respond. "Yes," I finally answer.

"If you wish to be alone, I will leave you during the days."

I don't really like the idea of being alone, but I'm not sure

I want to spend time in his company either. I swallow nervously and then reply, "Thank you."

His moods seem to change so suddenly, it's concerning. I've heard that Dragons are solitary creatures. Although they are able to shift forms, they are supposedly more beast than man, and it would seem this may be true. His social skills are sorely lacking in many regards.

I step forward and the sound of my steps change, telling me that this space is smaller than the long corridor, though not by much. This room is likely palatial. I open my mouth to speak but then quickly snap it shut when the door closes behind me, followed by the sound of his footsteps retreating down the hallway.

Sighing heavily, I cautiously extend my arm and begin to explore my room. Or my "chambers" as he called them. A crackling noise draws my attention and I skim my hand along the wall as I make my way toward it. The smell of burned wood and ash fills my nostrils as I approach what can only be a fireplace.

It seems my Dragon was kind enough to have a fire in here to warm the space, but I will need to figure out how to keep it burning. I run my hands along the stone mantel and find the tools to stoke the fire and a small stack of wood.

It's warm now, but I'm concerned about when it dies down. Fire is dangerous and I'm too afraid to add a log to a hearth that I am unfamiliar with and cannot see, worried that I'll somehow miss and end up setting the entire castle aflame.

I take a deep breath. This is something I will have to figure out later, I suppose. For now, I will continue exploring my room.

A different kind of warmth hits my skin and I cautiously reach out until I touch a smooth pane of glass. Tracing my fingers along the frame, I realize it is rather large. I trail my hand over the wall and when the smooth stone becomes rough wood beneath my fingers, I stop.

I find a handle and pull down on the latch. When I push the door open, a crisp saline breeze drifts in from outside, carrying the dull roar of the ocean with it. It is cold outside, but not unbearably so. I smile as the heat of the sun hits my face when I step through the door.

The floor beneath my feet sounds hollow as I venture farther out. I tap my left foot on the stone, making the hollow thud even louder. This must be a balcony of some sort.

The Dragon said this castle sits on a cliff. My stomach twists as I imagine myself falling over the edge and into the ocean below if I'm not careful. Taking a deep breath, I push down my fear. If I can live in a castle with an irritable and somewhat terrifying Dragon, I can handle anything.

When I discover the stone railing at the edge of the balcony, I'm satisfied it's tall enough that I won't accidentally fall over the side.

The cool wind whips through my hair and waves crash along the cliff wall below. I try to imagine what it all looks like, but I only ever saw the ocean once as a child when we traveled to a nearby kingdom for trade. I've always wanted to go back there, but now I never will.

Less than a year ago, a Dragon came to Solwyck—that kingdom's capital city—raining down fire and destruction upon the castle. Their princess managed to slay it, but at great cost to herself. They say she will never walk again.

I think about my own fate—first losing my parents and my sight, and now knowing that I have only one month to live. I suppose no one is immune to tragedy. Not even princesses.

When I walk back inside, I'm tired, but I need to clean myself up before I rest. Although Veron healed me, my hair is sticky with blood, and I can only imagine how I must appear. Surely there must be a cleansing room attached to this space. It is a castle after all.

I trace my hands along the wall until I find another door to the right of the bed. Wrapping my hand around the latch, I carefully push it open. A lovely floral scent fills the air as I step inside. Placing my hand on the wall, I count my steps as I learn the room, bumping first into a toilet and then into a sink. Farther along is a large tub already full of warm water.

A low bench against the tub has a folded towel. The fabric is plush and soft beneath my fingers. Beside it is a bottle of liquid. When I pull the cork from the top, the divine smell of lavender and jasmine hits my nose.

I'm not sure how all of this is here but it smells fresh and clean, so I quickly remove my clothing and cautiously lower myself into the water. Perhaps this was prepared in anticipation of my arrival by a servant. And yet, I have sensed no one else here save myself and Veron.

Warmth envelops me, soothing away all my tension as I sink beneath the surface and rinse my hair. Soaking in a heated bath is wonderful. If these are to be my final days, I plan to take advantage of this luxury every night that I am here.

When I am finished bathing, I walk back inside the main room and find the bed. Veron must spend much time in this space, for his scent is stronger here than in the rest of the castle. The smell of fresh rain and forest drifts up from the bedding and I wonder if perhaps he has given me *his* chambers to stay in while I'm here.

If so, I do not know if the idea is comforting or worrisome. But then I remember him saying that his people do not mate mine, so I know he will not force himself upon me. Perhaps this is his way of being kind.

Wherever he is, I hope he returns soon. The last month of

my life will be rather boring if I spend the entirety of it in this room. When he comes back, I will speak with him about going outside. If I can find something to use as a walking cane, I will have more freedom to explore and familiarize myself with my new surroundings.

Although he is a Dragon, perhaps we can find some common ground upon which to build some sort of companionship. I have never been one to enjoy solitude, and any company is preferable to none.

I have always believed that dying alone would be a terrible thing. Surely even a Dragon can understand that. Drawing in a deep breath, I decide that I will befriend Veron. Even if it's the last thing I do.

CHAPTER 4

VERON

I gave her my room. It is the first time I have done this in all these long years. She is a fragile creature. I could hardly believe how swollen her wrist was from a mere fall down the stairs.

When I felt the delicate bones beneath her skin as I healed her, it stirred something strange within me: a desire to watch over her. This odd feeling compelled me to give her my chambers. The fireplace in my bedroom is almost as large as the one in the great room downstairs. Winter is upon us. Someone so delicate surely needs to be kept warm during the cold nights, else I worry she will not survive the month.

She is... different from the ones before her. I can hardly believe that she asked to touch me. The others could barely stand to remain in my presence any longer than they absolutely had to.

Closing my eyes, I contemplate the feel of her skin against mine as she touched me. Her hair is the color of gold and her skin is petal soft. I clench my jaw as I recall how I had to stop her before her hands moved any farther down my body. My *stav* had already begun to extend from my mating pouch, as if I were about to mate her.

In truth, my body's response bothers me. How strange that I reacted so intensely to a human—a pitiful, weak race compared to my kind. Perhaps it is because I have lived apart from my people for so long that I am drawn to another, regardless of our differences.

We Dragons are solitary creatures, but we still interact from time to time with one another. My curse prevents me from seeking company, however. Only during the blood moon am I able to shift into my two-legged form and think clearly. For the rest of the year, the curse shrouds my mind in a fog, and I am forced to remain in my Dragon form and unable to think beyond my beastly instincts.

It is a cruel punishment to take away my logic and reason in this way. That is why I both long for and dread the blood moon cycle in equal measure. It is the only time I may freely shift forms and the only time I am truly myself.

However, I dislike spending that time in the company of a human. I suppose the witch considered this condition yet another facet of my torture, knowing how much my people despise their race.

But if I want to remain myself as long as possible, I must ensure the human—*Alara*—is comfortable. If she tries to run away or end her life to escape whatever unspeakable fate she believes I hold in store for her, I will revert to my Dragon form. The heavy fog of the curse will blanket my thoughts; I will lose all my memories and be little more than a beast for the rest of the year.

It has been so long I have lost count of the years of my torture. The faces of my captives all blur together after a time. I can remember them if I focus, but this one, somehow, is different. Something about her fascinates me and I do not understand why. Perhaps it is because, despite her fragile form, she is brave. A quality that is usually found lacking in her race.

I think back on all the humans before her who cried almost the entire time they were here. But this female? She has not cried even once in my presence. She even inquired about breaking the curse. Her question surprised me, for she is the first one to have ever asked.

I have attempted, in the past, to break it without involving my captives. I tried to kill myself, but the blood magic brought me back the next morning. I even set one woman free, which triggered a backlash so terrible, I instantly morphed into a mindless, destructive beast. I razed her entire village to the ground along with several surrounding towns before the blood magic was satisfied that I'd been punished enough for trying to cheat the curse.

It is well-known my kind are one of the most powerful of the otherworldly realm. Little did I know how much power a blood witch possesses as well. I did not truly believe she could curse me as she did. It seems the magic of a blood witch is one of the few that is stronger than my people.

As I wait for the invisible staff of the castle to prepare a meal for Alara and myself, I walk out to the gardens. Lost in my memories and regrets, I make my way to the rosebush without thinking. It keeps time with the blood moon cycle. I stare down at the vibrant red blooms in dismay. Thirty days is how long they will stay. When the last petal falls, Alara will turn to stone just like the rest. And I will become an unthinking brute once again.

As if my very thoughts have summoned her, the witch appears in my path. I am used to her coming and going in such a way, so her sudden appearance does not startle me.

Her amber eyes meet mine, and a smirk twists her mouth

as her gaze drops to the rosebush. "What poor maiden did they offer you this time?"

Instead of answering, I scowl as a low growl rumbles deep in my chest. Fire licks at the back of my throat with the desire to shift forms and burn her to ash. But she is powerful and clever, this witch, and she would be gone before I even opened my mouth.

She tips her head to the side, regarding me with a piercing gaze. An evil grin curls her lips. "Tell me: Do you believe that this will be the one to break your curse?"

My claws lengthen into sharpened points as I imagine rending the flesh from her bones. One day, I vow that I will break free. And when I do, I will end her, but not before I make her suffer for having cursed me.

Her mocking laugh taunts me. "The girl intrigues you. I saw it when you first arrived back at the castle."

I clench my jaw. I hate that this foul creature can spy upon me at all times without me knowing.

She continues. "Already you are beginning to change, you know. One day it will happen. And you will truly understand what you took from me. You will learn about heartache and loss, and it will destroy you completely."

"Is that the point of all this?" I flare my nostrils. "Because if it is, you are wasting your time."

"Am I?" She sneers.

I meet her gaze evenly. "Dragons do not love. Matters of the heart do not affect us."

Fire burns in her eyes as she sidles closer. "Mark my words. Some day you will learn what it is to love. And when you do, you will understand what you took from me. For I will make certain the thing you cherish most is taken from you as well. Dragons have long lives, and I will ensure yours is filled with an ocean of pain and regret by the time this is done."

Without warning, she vanishes just as quickly as she first appeared. I loathe the blood witch. She thinks she will change me, but she is wrong. Dragons do not love.

CHAPTER 5

VERON

When I take the evening meal to Alara's room, I am careful to knock and remind her to make certain her blindfold is on before she answers the door. It would not do to have her turn to stone so early in our... arrangement.

She greets me with her blindfold in place and a nervous smile. Her long, golden hair is slightly damp, as if she has freshly bathed. I move past her and place her food upon the table. Once I am finished, I turn to leave, but her words pull me up short. "You're not staying?"

Slowly, I spin to face her. "You... wish me to stay?"

"Yes."

My curiosity is piqued. "Why?"

"Because I'd like to get to know you. And I'm not used to eating alone."

"The others preferred to be left alone."

"Well, I'm... different."

I arch a brow. "Yes, I'm starting to see that."

I take a seat across from her and watch as she carefully traces her fingers over the plate and utensils before eating. She is very careful and methodical in her movements. I'm surprised she wishes me to remain here when it would probably be much easier for her to eat her meal without a blindfold.

"Did you make this meal?"

"No. The castle provided it. It is enchanted."

Her brows shoot up to her forehead. "Enchanted?"

"Yes. I can neither see nor hear any servants. I only know that everything gets done as if they were here. Meals are prepared and then the plates and silverware cleaned after I've eaten. Baths are drawn and fresh towels are left out. Linens are changed, clothing is provided... all is kept neat and tidy, as if taken care of each day by hidden staff."

She tips her head slightly to the side as if listening for something. "Are you not eating?"

"I will hunt later."

She lowers her fork. "Hunt?"

"Yes. There is plenty of game to be had in the forest outside the castle."

"But... I thought the castle provided you with whatever you needed."

"It does. But I prefer to hunt."

"My father was a hunter as well." A wistful smile crests her lips. "He was so skilled with a bow that we never went hungry while he was alive."

"Was? Your father is gone?"

She nods. "He died during the last plague that swept through the kingdom."

She has been through much, it seems. My gaze travels over her slight form. It is easy to see she is no stranger to hunger. "Food is not scarce here. You may eat as much as you like," I inform her. "As I mentioned before, the castle is enchanted and will provide whatever you need."

She purses her lips. "What about dessert?"

"The kitchen will provide that as well."

She tilts her head. "Do Dragons eat dessert?"

"No. We do not like sweet things."

A hint of a grin curls her mouth. "Then, I guess I'll be forced to eat yours as well, so it won't go to waste."

Despite my best efforts, a smile tugs my lips at her teasing. She amuses me. This human is strange and yet... I find myself curious to know more about her.

*　*　*

When she finishes dinner, I bid her good evening so I may go to hunt. As I open the door, her soft voice makes me pause. "Veron?"

I turn around to face her. "Yes?"

"Be careful while you're out."

I frown. Does she think me weak? "I am a Dragon. We are not easily killed."

"I know. But no one is invincible."

"You would not be... happy if something tragic were to befall me?" I ask, curious to understand her logic.

"Why would I be glad if you were hurt or killed?" Her small brow furrows deeply. "What kind of person do you think I am?"

My head jerks back slightly in surprise. All the others could barely tolerate my presence. Every time I came near them, they would stink of fear and begin crying, even after I assured them I meant no harm. I study Alara curiously.

"Well?" she asks, and I realize I have not answered her question.

"An odd one," I finally reply.

Her mouth drifts open slightly, but I do not wait for her to speak. Instead, I leave her room and head down the hallway. My muscles are already rippling beneath the surface of my scales, longing to shift forms.

As soon as I step outside, I close my eyes and allow the transformation to take over. My Dragon form is ever ready just beneath the surface, like a wild and untamed thing waiting to be freed. To shift is one of the greatest joys imaginable.

A thrill runs through me as I breathe in the fresh, cold air and spread my wings. The deep stretch as they unfold from my body is a feeling unlike any other. Staring up at the gray and overcast sky, I lift off and climb above the trees.

From up here, the ocean stretches out along the horizon to my left and the dark forest to the right. I turn and head for the woods, flying low.

My nostrils flare as I scent for any prey. In the darkness, I am able to see clearly. Several deer up ahead draw my attention, but they are an easy kill, and I would prefer a challenge this night.

Something about Alara's words bothered me. If a female Dragon were to express such concern for my safety, it would mean she believed me incapable of defending myself.

No female Dragon would ever consider a male for a mate if she thought he was weak in any way. But Alara is not a Dragon. Her words and her opinion should hold no weight with me. Certainly not in this way. How can such a fragile creature have the audacity to question my ability to defend, protect, and provide for myself?

I fly close to the castle, wondering if she is still awake. There is no risk if she is and happens to see me in this form. There is only a danger of her turning to stone if she views me in my two-legged state.

As I approach her balcony, the soft light from the window

draws my attention. Quietly, I set down on the ledge outside and peer in. The fireplace has enough wood stacked on the hearth to keep the flames burning all night long to keep her warm. I stoked it earlier so it will not die down while she sleeps.

I scan the room and find her asleep on the bed. Her long, silken hair spreads out beneath her on the pillow like a beautiful, golden halo; her thick lashes fan over flawless, pink cheeks; and her lips part in a small, round O. The light of the fire casts her flaxen hair in a heavenly glow, making her appear almost ethereal—angelic as she sleeps. Curling my claws reflexively into my palm, I struggle against the desire to shift forms and go to her.

I have never seen anything more beautiful.

Inexplicably drawn to her, I long to feel the brush of her skin against my own. But I push this thought aside. I am disturbed by my intense fascination with Alara, and I force my eyes to look away from her sleeping form.

Not wanting to think about her any longer, I lift off the balcony and take to the skies. The cold air burns my lungs with each inhalation as snowflakes twirl and dance on the crisp, saline breeze. I head out toward the forest, scanning the darkness as I search for my prey.

Dark and primal instincts take over as I lose myself to the hunt.

* * *

AFTER MY THIRD KILL, my blood lust is finally sated. I bathe in a stream near the edge of the woods, washing the blood from my scales before I fly back to the castle.

Humans may not possess a heightened sense of smell like my kind, but I've learned they are able to scent blood rather easily and I do not wish to frighten Alara when I return.

I take the rooms next to hers—the ones I had originally intended as her chambers. I lie down upon the bed, but I cannot sleep. Staring up at the ceiling, I lift my hand to my face and touch my lips, remembering how she traced them with her delicate fingers.

Why does this human fascinate me so? The way she touched me, spoke to me, practically demanded that I describe the world to her... she has a strength of will and a bravery that is equal to that of a Dragon. It makes me curious about her, I suppose. For the first time in all the long years of my curse, I am eager for morning to come.

Once I have spent more time with Alara, perhaps I will understand why she intrigues me so.

CHAPTER 6

VERON

When morning comes, I fight the urge to knock on her door. I am hesitant to wake her if she is still asleep. Her kind tire easily and I want her mind to be sharp when we are together, for I wish to understand its inner workings. The best way to get to know her is through intelligent conversation.

I slip inside the hidden door in the hallway and make my way down the secret passageway to her room—my room, technically.

Coveting the silver-capped domes of the castle, I stole this palace from its original inhabitants many years ago. I have often wondered what use they had for these hidden spaces, and this is the first time I have taken advantage of them.

I slide back the hidden panel and peer into the room. She is standing by the window in her sleeping gown, staring out at the sea. The wind blows through her hair, gently tussling the long, golden strands and carrying her delicate scent on the breeze.

Winter is upon us, bringing the colder air with it. A light blanket of snow covers the ground all around the estate, except for the gardens, which remain evergreen due to the castle's enchantment.

I worry Alara will catch cold if she remains outside for very long in so little clothing. If she dies before the last petal falls from the rosebush, I will be forced back into my Dragon form all that much sooner, and unable to shift until the next blood moon cycle.

But that is not the only reason I am concerned for her well-being. Something about her intrigues me. I cannot help but want to understand her better. Even knowing her as little as I do, I am discomforted at the thought of her turning to stone.

I am glad that I did not knock on the door, for she is not wearing her blindfold right now. When she turns and places her hand on the wall, I catch sight of her deep, sapphire-blue eyes.

I watch her take a few hesitant steps, counting as she goes.

I frown. Her gaze is fixed on the wall ahead, yet it seems unfocused, as if she stares at nothing. When she reaches the wardrobe, she runs her hands over the doors, pulling them open when her fingers find the handle. She reaches in and strokes the fabric of each dress before selecting one.

She stretches up on her toes to pull the garment from its hanger. I observe curiously as she places her hand on the wall and begins counting again as she walks back to the bed.

Her behavior is odd, but then again, humans are strange, pitiful creatures. Perhaps she feels weak because she has not eaten yet, so she needs the wall to steady herself.

Morning light filters in through the window, outlining

her body beneath the silken material of her sleeping gown. She is smaller than a female Dragon in two-legged form. It is strange that her people have skin instead of scales. How do they defend themselves from harm with such a weak covering over their bodies?

Her gown accents the sensuous curve of her breasts, where a Dragon female would be flat. Her waist is so small, my hands could easily circle it. The gentle flare of her hips and the rounded curve of her backside are oddly appealing.

I shake my head to clear my errant thoughts. I should not be thinking of a human in this way. It Is undignified.

I slip back out into the hallway, heading downstairs to arrange food for our breakfast. She must eat and gather her strength; it will not do to have her too feeble to spend time with me after she already expressed a desire to do so.

Our time is limited, and I wish to explore her mind while she is here. If for no other reason than to find out why she differs from her predecessors.

CHAPTER 7

ALARA

I am glad the cleansing room is attached to my chambers instead of down the hall, like it was in my home with Lilly. It makes it easy to ready myself this morning to start my day. I pull a dress from the wardrobe and quickly slip it on, marveling at the silken feel of the fabric against my skin.

It is cold this morning, and the fire has burned down to mere embers, but I am hesitant to stoke the flame or add more wood to the hearth. I would rather not risk accidentally setting fire to the castle. Perhaps I can ask Veron to do this for me later.

Wrapping my blindfold around my head, I open the door and step out into the hallway.

"Veron?" I call out, wondering if he's awake.

He went hunting last night, and I wonder if he returned or if he's still asleep. When I don't hear a reply, I continue. Counting the steps to the top of the staircase, I place my hand on the banister to steady myself and carefully descend to the first floor.

Veron said the castle provides whatever he needs, and I'm hoping it will produce some sort of breakfast for me because I woke up rather hungry this morning. I'm not entirely sure where the kitchen is, but maybe I'll find my Dragon host downstairs and he can direct me.

When I reach the first floor, I call out to him again, but there is no answer.

I place my hand on the wall and cautiously follow it, hoping it will lead me to the kitchen. If nothing else, I can familiarize myself with the downstairs level so I can have more confidence when moving about the castle. A walking cane would be ideal for exploring my surroundings, and I once again lament that I had to leave mine behind.

When I reach a large set of doors, I carefully push them open, hoping to find the kitchen behind them. The groan of the hinges reverberates loudly, telling me that this space is sizable. I continue for a bit, but stop when I realize that this is most likely a long hallway of some sort. I have yet to find any furnishings or doors along this wall.

A small frisson of fear travels up my spine as I think of Veron's warning about the west wing. What if that's what this is? I've walked dozens of steps and not found anything yet, and I worry that I've accidentally wandered into the one place he forbade me to go.

Quickly, I turn around and start back the way I came, hoping that I'll reach the great room before Veron returns from wherever he is.

Counting my steps under my breath, I'm panting heavily as I rush back to the large doors, frantic to return to the great room. My palms are damp, and I can hear nothing over my pulse drumming in my ears as I make my way down the long hallway.

An ear-splitting roar shatters the silence. My veins fill with ice and I still as thunderous footsteps move toward me. A deep and menacing growl echoes along the stone walls, striking terror in my heart. "This is the west wing. Why are you in here?"

Through my trembling lips, I somehow speak. "I got lost. I—"

"Get out of here!" he bellows.

Frantic to escape, I press my shaking hand to the wall and stumble forward. Panic spikes through me as I rush down the hallway. In my panicked retreat, I trip over the carpet, barely managing to catch myself before I fall, losing my blindfold in the process.

Slamming my palm again to the stone for guidance, I force myself to my feet. I have to get out of here. Now!

Warm air blows across my face and I squeeze my eyes shut. I sweep my hand out and hit something solid. Overwhelming fear lends speed to my steps as I scramble around it and keep going.

"Alara!" Veron's thunderous voice calls out, but I do not stop, and I dare not turn back.

I push through the door and keep my hand on the wall until I find the banister. Panicked, I lose count halfway up the stairs and stumble forward at the top, hitting my head so hard on the wall I cannot tell which way is up or down. Breathing in and out through pursed lips, I blink back tears as I steady myself.

Loud footsteps on the stairs spike fear in my chest. Mustering the last of my strength, I race down the long corridor to my room. When I reach it, I slam the door shut behind me. Hastily, I count my way to the table and chairs and then drag them back to the door to block it.

A loud pounding on the wood stops my heart. "Alara! Open this door!"

"No!"

"Open. This. Door." Veron growls low in his throat. "Now."

"No!"

The hinges creak and groan from the force of his assault, and I back away on shaky legs. "Leave me alone!"

"Fine!" he yells through the door, and then I hear him stomp down the hallway, away from my room.

My heart is pounding as I sit on the edge of the bed, trying to force myself to calm down. Tears sting my eyes, and despite my best attempts to keep them in, the first one escapes my lashes and rolls softly down my cheek.

I miss my home and my sister. And without my walking cane, I feel so lost. Veron was so angry, it was terrifying. He didn't even let me explain.

A broken sob leaves my throat, and tears track down my face as devastation wells up within. I drop my head into my hands. Is this how it's going to be here? Must I remain locked up in my room until I fade away at the end of the blood moon cycle?

Collapsing back onto the bed, I bury my face in my pillow and release all the tears and pain I've been holding in since the day my sister was first chosen as the sacrifice. I wouldn't allow myself to cry then because I didn't want Lilly to know how afraid I was for her. But now that it's just me, I no longer care. I'm miserable here and soon I will die.

I bite my lower lip to stop it from trembling. I thought I was strong enough to do this, but now I'm not so sure. Curling my hands into fists, I press them into the pillow to still their shaking.

Clenching my jaw, I draw in a deep, shuddering breath. This was my decision to take Lilly's place and come in her stead. I sniff and wipe at my tears, forcing myself to stop crying. I am stronger than this. I have to be if I'm going to survive until the end of the blood moon cycle.

Rolling onto my side, I pull the blanket over my shoulders. I send a silent prayer to the heavens, thanking the gods and my parents that my sister at least will never suffer this dark fate. As I fall away into sleep, I draw comfort from the knowledge that my sacrifice will give her the chance to live a beautiful life with her beloved.

CHAPTER 8

VERON

Alara is blind. She lied to me. She has been wearing the blindfold all this time, but when it fell from her eyes, she merely blinked. Fear stopped my heart, and for a moment I could not move. The curse turns anyone who views me in my two-legged form to stone. But she stared straight at my face, and she did not see me at all. Instead, she raced away, locking me out of her room.

Even as I consider this, anger fills me anew. Not only has she been keeping secrets from me, but she also defied my command. I found her in the west wing—the one place I forbade her to go.

I step outside and shift into my Dragon form. Flexing my wings, I launch into the sky and fly high over the castle.

How dare this human defy me. Who does she think she is?

I must speak with Alara, but not while the fire of my anger still burns bright within. Spreading my wings, I catch the wind in my sails and slip into the current as I glide out over the ocean. The crisp saline air fills my lungs with each breath. There is something about the sea that always calms me when I am upset.

After a while my anger dissipates, and I head back to the shoreline. The light from Alara's window is dim and I swoop low, curious to know what she is doing.

It has been several hours since she locked herself in her room, refusing to allow me inside. I am a Dragon. She must understand that while she is here, she will do as I say. I will not have her ignoring my orders and exploring parts of the castle that I've expressly told her are forbidden.

It is fortunate that I discovered her before she had gone too far. If she knew what awaited her in the west wing, she would truly be afraid, and I do not want that for her.

Carefully, I settle on her balcony and then peer inside. The fire has dwindled down to mere embers. As I sweep my gaze over the room, I notice her lying in bed, shivering beneath the covers.

What foolishness is this? Does she mean to freeze herself to death just to get away from me? Why has she not kept the fire going?

Angered that she ignored my orders and went into the west wing, locked me out of my own room, and is now trying to kill herself by freezing, I push the balcony door open. She jerks up in the bed. Her eyes are wide and unseeing as she whips her head toward the sound of my footsteps. "Veron?"

"Why have you not kept the fire going?" I demand.

"What are you doing in my room?"

"Answer me," I demand.

"No," she snaps, standing from the bed. "*You* answer me!"

My jaw drops. Stunned by her blatant defiance, I stand there frozen in place. Is she intentionally yelling at me? I open my mouth to speak, but she cuts me off.

"That's it! I've had enough of your sour moods, Veron. I understand that you've been cursed, and you're trapped and miserable here, but that doesn't mean you have to take your anger out on me."

"I—"

"I got lost today. That's how I ended up in the west wing. But you didn't even let me explain."

It is comforting to know she was not deliberately disobeying my instructions, but I'm uncertain how to respond to this blatant defiance she is exhibiting now. How does she think she can speak to me this way? Has she completely forgotten what I am?

She lifts her hand, pointing an accusing finger in my direction. "And rather than listen to what I had to say, you turned into an angry, fire-breathing Dragon. Do you have any idea how terrified I was?"

I arch a brow. If she is anything like her fellow humans, I would imagine she probably feared for her life. I am a Dragon; that is to be expected, unless my long years trapped here have made me soft.

She spreads her arms wide. "So, if you're here to kill me, then just get it over with." She gestures exaggeratedly. "I'm not going to live in fear while I'm trapped here with you."

My mouth drifts open. She would rather die than live afraid? I had no idea humans were this brave. Or… perhaps it is foolishness, or some temporary form of insanity. I am uncertain.

Squeezing her eyes shut, she clenches her jaw and rasps. "Just do it. Get it over with already. I'm tired of waiting."

I scoff. This human is unbelievable. With a heavy sigh, I run a hand through my hair as I study her. She is either foolish, brave, or insane. I cannot tell which it is as she stands there, waiting for me to end her life. "I am not going to kill you. My vow."

"You're not?" she asks, and it is easy to read the surprise in her expression.

"No."

She crosses her arms over her chest. "Then, apologize."

My head jerks back. *"What?"*

"Apologize to me and promise you will not lose your temper like that again while I'm here."

I blink at her in astonishment. This weak and fragile human is demanding that a Dragon apologize to her? Is she serious?

"Well?" she asks, tapping her foot impatiently against the stone floor.

"Fine," I grumble.

She scowls, still appearing displeased. "Is that your idea of an apology?"

"I…" I am dumbfounded. "What do you expect me to say?"

She huffs out a frustrated breath. "How about 'I'm sorry and I promise not to turn into an angry, fire-breathing Dragon again while you're here.'"

"This is ridiculous. I cannot promise such a thing."

"Why not?"

"Because I *am* a fire-breathing Dragon."

"Yes, but you do not have to be an *angry* one," she counters. "Now, apologize or else leave me be."

I blink several times. She *is* serious about this. This *human* is demanding I apologize to *her*? My gaze travels over her form. She may be small, but she is as fierce as a Dragon female.

I am completely enthralled.

Crossing the room in three strides, I drop to one knee. "I am sorry."

"And?" she demands.

I snort. "I cannot vow not to turn into something that I

already *am*. What if an enemy storms the castle while you are here? Am I supposed to pretend I am not a Dragon, and greet them in a friendly manner?"

She sighs. "No, I suppose not."

I arch a brow as I stare up at her. "Is my apology good enough *now*?"

She tips her chin up in an imperious look. "It will do."

I stand and then blink down at her, studying her intently. "Why did you not tell me you were blind?"

"I thought you would be mad."

Confused by her reply, I'm about to ask her what she means, but she interrupts me and gestures toward the fireplace. "You asked me about the fire. I let it burn low because I was worried I might miss the hearth if I added more wood. I did not want to risk placing a log too close to the carpets and accidentally setting fire to the castle."

An uncomfortable knot forms in my stomach. Upset at myself for not realizing her lack of sight would make it difficult for her to keep the fire going, I add more wood to the hearth and stoke the embers until they burn brightly once more.

She shivers slightly and the strange knot in my stomach grows even more uncomfortable. "I have restarted the fire," I tell her. "It should warm the room soon."

"Thank you," she murmurs.

I don't miss the way her teeth chatter as she speaks.

I pull the blanket from the bed and wrap it around her shoulders. "You said you got lost this morning. What were you looking for?"

"I was hungry."

Now I feel even worse. She was hungry this morning; it is nighttime, and she has had nothing to eat the entire day. I must remedy this at once.

I move to her door, pulling the table and chairs away so I

can open it. As soon as it's clear, I hurry out into the hallway and down to the kitchen for food. With each step, my discomfort grows even more. Why do I feel this way? What is it about this human that vexes me so? Why should I care if she is cold? Hungry?

Part of me still cannot believe I apologized to her.

Yes, I want her to live out all the days permitted by the curse because I do not want to return to a mindless beast. But it is more than that. I am experiencing a physical reaction of... unpleasantness of some sort at the mere thought of her being in discomfort.

I do not want her to fear me either. With all the others, it did not matter. But she is different, and it frustrates me that I do not understand why.

When I reach the kitchen, a bowl of soup and a small loaf of bread are already waiting for me on the counter. Steam rises from the bowl as if it were freshly prepared. Which, I suppose it was. Even though I do not understand the enchantment of this place, it is rather convenient. The only positive thing to come from this curse.

I quickly make my way back to her room and find her seated before the fire, still wrapped up in her blanket. I know she has already heard my return when her head turns in my direction.

"Veron?" she says softly. "You came back?"

"I brought you some food."

I sit down next to her, carefully handing her the bowl of soup and bread. I grit my teeth in frustration when I realize I've not brought her a spoon. "I forgot the utensils. I'll be right back."

Her small hand on my forearm stops me abruptly. "It's all right. I'll just use the bread."

I watch her break a small piece off and dip it into the soup. When she places it in her mouth, a low appreciative hum rises in her throat as she chews. "This is delicious," she murmurs.

I study her a moment, and then ask my question again. "Why did you keep your blindness a secret?"

She turns to me. "How did you know?"

"When I found you in the west wing, I was in my two-legged form, and you did not see me even as I stood before you. If you had, you would have turned to stone. Why would you not tell me that you are unable to see?"

"I was afraid you would reject me as the sacrifice."

"How long have you been this way?"

"The last plague took my parents and my sight eight years ago."

Her eyelids blink several times as she stares straight ahead, her gaze fixed but unfocused. Up close, I study her luminous eyes. "Blue as sapphire gemstones," I whisper more to myself than to her.

"My mother's eyes were the same." She smiles. "My sister, Lilly—her eyes are brown like my father's were." She lowers her head. "You are not upset that I lied to you?"

"No," I admit as I continue to stare at her curiously. "You fascinate me." The words escape my mouth unfiltered and I move to correct myself. "What I meant is—"

A faint smile curves her mouth. "You are fascinated with me?"

Angry at myself for voicing this aloud, I change the subject. "Do you have any family left?"

She nods. "All I have now is my sister, Lilly, and her fiancé, Garen. My best friend, Mara, came here to be with you last year. Do you—do you remember her?"

I close my eyes. I may not particularly like humans, but I do pity them their fate when they come to my castle. "I remember them all," I admit. "We did not spend much time together. She preferred to be alone while she was here."

She takes my hand in hers, squeezing it gently as tears brighten her eyes. "Thank you for respecting her wishes, then. I'm sure she appreciated it."

I am both surprised and moved that she would thank me for such basic decency. After all, is it not my fault these humans are cursed?

She continues. "My sister was supposed to be the sacrifice this year, but I took her place so she could marry Garen."

Anger sparks to life in my chest. How could her sister allow Alara to take her place? "Your sister made you come to me in her stead so she could marry?"

She shakes her head. "It was my choice. She did not know."

Ah. That makes sense. I study her with renewed admiration. Alara is very brave.

"I am glad my sister will live." She blinks back tears. "She and Garen took care of me after our parents died. They helped me learn how to navigate the world without my sight."

"I imagine it must have been a difficult adjustment," I offer.

"It was," she agrees. "But it wasn't just the loss of my vision that was hard to accept, it was all that came with it."

"What do you mean?"

"Most people treat me as if I'm some sort of broken thing instead of a person. When we'd go to the market, I would hear some of the villagers whispering about how I was pretty, but I'd never find a husband who would accept me without my sight." She swallows hard. "It was… difficult to hear such things. To be so harshly judged for my blindness instead of acknowledged for who I truly am."

Anger twists deep inside me and a puff of smoke curls out from my nostrils. Alara is selfless and braver than any human

I have ever met. "The people of your village are small-minded fools."

"I suspect many of them simply do not know any better." She shrugs. "That's why my father encouraged us to always keep an open mind. He said many people live in ignorance of all they do not know." She pauses. "I mean, I used to believe that all Dragons are dangerous."

"We are."

She cocks her head to one side. "Are you suggesting I should be afraid of you?"

Fierce protectiveness floods my veins as I study her. "I would never harm you, Alara."

A lovely smile curves her mouth and I stare at her, completely transfixed. She is a rare and precious jewel among her kind.

As we sit together by the fire, we continue to chat amiably. I do not know why I desire to know so much about her. But despite my better judgment, I am most curious to find out.

CHAPTER 9

VERON

It has been nine days since Alara came to be here with me and we have established a routine. Every morning, I bring her breakfast to begin our day. She tells me stories about her life, and I share mine with her. It is strange how much I find myself looking forward to these exchanges.

When I reach the kitchen, I already know that when I enter, the food will have been prepared and waiting. I'm surprised, however, when I open the doors to find our breakfast packed neatly in a wicker basket with a blanket to spread out on the ground as if for a picnic.

It is strange how the castle can read my mind, for I had been thinking of having first meal in the gardens this morning. Although I do not understand how the enchantment of the castle works, I also have lived with it for so many years that I no longer question it.

I take the basket out to the gardens and spread the blanket on the grass. Although it is winter beyond the castle, you'd never know it here. The gardens are warm, and every plant is in full bloom as if it were springtime. It is only this way when I have… a guest. The rest of the year, the gardens are bleak and dead.

When I'm finished laying out our picnic, I return inside and then knock on her door.

"I'll be right there," she calls out in a singsong voice.

When she opens the door, she greets me with a lovely smile. "Good morning."

I am surprised at how carefree she seems this morning. When was the last time a human stood before a Dragon without fear? I admire Alara for her bravery. She is as fierce as a female of my kind.

"Are you hungry?"

She nods, reaching out her hand. I take it in mine and carefully guide her through the castle. Under her breath, she begins counting.

She does this everywhere we go, and I understand it is so that she can learn her surroundings and be able to find her way around the castle without me if she needs to. She has expressed a desire for something she refers to as a walking cane, stating that such an item will help her navigate her way with more confidence.

I've promised her we will go into the forest today to retrieve some wood suitable for this purpose. I want her to have as much freedom as possible while she is here.

While she is here. The words are like bitter acid on my tongue. I dare not speak them aloud, for they remind me she will be gone soon, just like all the others.

"What's wrong?" she asks, ripping me from my dark thoughts.

"Nothing," I lie.

"Something is wrong." She arches a brow. "What is it?"

"How do you know?"

A smile touches the corners of her mouth. "Normally, I

would not share this because anyone would think me mad. But"—her carefree expression falters—"that doesn't matter now. So, I will tell you, no matter how strange it may sound. To me, a colorful aura surrounds each person, and the color tells me their mood."

"I do not understand."

"I don't *see* the color... I can *feel* it. If that makes sense."

It does not, but I wait patiently for her to continue.

"Your color a moment ago was gray, telling me that you felt melancholy."

It is the truth. I was depressed thinking of how short a time we have left. However, I remain quiet, reluctant to admit this. She knows our days together are limited. I recall the other captives, how distraught they became whenever they were reminded of their imminent fate.

For some reason, I detest the idea of upsetting her in this way.

She reaches for my other hand, turning my body to face her fully. She tips her chin up, as if she could meet my eyes. "You are a Dragon. One of the most powerful beings in existence. How did you come to be cursed?"

Does she suggest I am weak because this happened to me? "Why do you wish to know?"

She tips her head to the side. "I am curious."

Ah. So, it seems she is just as curious about me as I am about her. This obsession, I understand. "I tried to steal the treasure hoard of a blood witch."

Her brows shoot up to her forehead. "Why would you do such a thing?"

I shrug. "I am a Dragon. We cannot resist treasure. And hers was the largest I had ever seen."

"So, what happened?"

I hesitate a moment, reluctant to tell her. Before Alara, I would not have cared about a human's opinion. But I do not want her to know the truth for fear she will judge me harshly for it. So, I offer her a half truth. "As I said before, I stole from the blood witch and she caught me."

The part of my story that I leave out is that the witch's mate died when I burned my way through her castle to steal her treasure. And because the people of the city surrounding her estate shot their pitiful arrows at me, I razed it to the ground, burning it to ash with my Dragon fire. They dared offer resistance, and I wanted to teach them a lesson.

No one gets between a Dragon and the treasure they covet.

"I don't understand. Why would she curse you like this over treasure? Why make it so that the curse can only be broken when someone can look upon you and see their true love?"

I clench my jaw. "She said she wanted me to understand loneliness, loss, and such. So, she created this curse, knowing it would never be broken."

"How do you know it will never be broken?"

"Why would a human have such affection for me? They fear Dragons. Besides… my kind do not love."

"Oh," she says. Her lips purse thoughtfully. "Are you saying that Dragons do not take mates?"

A small puff of air escapes me. "On the contrary. We mate for life. But it is about claim and possession. Not love." I pause. "So, now you understand why my curse can never be undone."

Her small hand squeezes mine. "I am sorry."

I do not understand why she apologizes for that which cannot be her fault. It is strange, yet oddly comforting.

"I have a request," she announces.

I narrow my eyes, wondering what she means to ask of me. She already knows I cannot let her go. "What is it?"

"I understand your kind normally appreciate their solitude, but… would you mind spending time with me? While I'm here."

While she is here. Why do these words pierce my heart? I do not understand.

She continues. "Humans enjoy—even crave—the company of others. I know I do not have much time left, and I'd rather not spend it alone. Is that all right with you?"

It is what we have already been doing anyway. To be completely honest, I am happy to grant her this; I wish to spend every day studying this strange female that captivates me so. "I will do as you ask."

A brilliant smile lights her face, revealing two rows of flat white teeth instead of fangs. I wonder how her people mark their mates to claim them. It seems impossible that such blunt tools could pierce flesh.

"Thank you," she breathes. "I'd rather spend my last days full of companionship and happiness rather than dwelling on what I cannot change."

A strange lump forms in my throat. I admire her strength of will. "If this is what you wish, then that is what we will do."

"Alright, then." She gives me another dazzling smile. "What shall we do today?"

"We will start with breakfast in the gardens."

I enjoy the outside and I know many of the others before her did as well. We have not spent any time in the gardens before now, partly because I am loath to see the rosebush, reminding me how short our time together is.

"That sounds lovely," she replies. "What an excellent idea."

I lead her out into the gardens where I've already spread a blanket and laid out the food. Carefully, I guide her to sit beside me and then hand her a plate with her breakfast. I intend to keep my human well fed during our time together.

When she takes the first bite of her fruit, an appreciative sound hums in the back of her throat. "These berries are wonderful. How did you come by these in the middle of winter?"

I am pleased she likes them. "The enchantment upon this land keeps the gardens in constant springtime."

Her mouth drifts open. "That sort of magic is hardly a curse. It sounds wonderful. To have things taken care of with no effort."

I nod. "All magic, even blood magic, must have a balance. For every curse, there is also a blessing."

She smiles. "No wonder it smells so incredible out here. Are the flowers all in full bloom?"

"Yes."

"Will you give me a tour of the gardens when we're done?"

"Of course."

I wonder at her desiring this, for it is not as if she can see any of the plants or flowers to enjoy them.

After she finishes her food, she takes my hand, and we walk arm in arm through the gardens. An oddly possessive feeling unfurls deep within me as she touches me effortlessly, as if she has nothing to fear.

"Describe the gardens to me," she reminds me. "I'd love to know what they look like."

I allow my gaze to drift over the landscape. "We are on one of several winding pathways. A small stream runs throughout, intersecting the path here and there. Several flowering bushes, dotted with various purple, blue, and red blooms, are scattered along the way. Vines laden with small, budding white flowers trail over the garden wall. They sway gently in the breeze like living curtains.

"Several large, gray oaks are surrounded by a thick blanket of lush grass. They twist up toward the sky, reaching for the sunlight. Up ahead, do you hear the sound of water?"

She nods.

"Carved into the side of the mountain, a small waterfall of crystal-clear water spills down a series of stacked gray stones into a pool below. It is surprisingly warm, and I believe it is because of the enchantment of this place."

"Do you ever swim here?"

"No." In truth, the idea never occurred to me.

She turns to me with a grin. "Then we must add swimming to our list of things to do while I'm here."

"You are strange." The admission leaves my mouth before I can contain it.

"So are you," she teases. "That's why I believe we get along so well."

"Why is that?"

"Because we are used to others finding us strange, we've become more tolerant of other odd people."

I arch a brow. "Your reasoning is sound."

"Thank you." Her lips curve into a stunning smile that stops my heart momentarily.

I am completely mesmerized as I study her face. She is the most beautiful person I have ever seen.

"Are you able to live in the castle when you are in Dragon form?"

"No. I stay... elsewhere."

She does not press for any further details. We continue through the garden until she suddenly stops.

Curious, I watch her turn and reach for the rosebush with her free hand. "This smells lovely," she says. Her fingers skim lightly across one of the vibrant red blooms and my breath catches.

She has found the cursed plant—the one that keeps time with the moon.

The roses only bloom during the blood moon cycle, the flowers waning with each passing day until finally, it wilts completely. Once the last petal falls, our time will be through, and she will turn to stone.

"You've grown sad again," she says softly, pulling me back from my dark thoughts. "Why?"

I do not know if it is her fate that saddens me or the prospect of being forced into my Dragon form to be alone once more. To be cut off from the world and my own people is a horrible way to live.

But as I stare at her, I realize that losing her will be even worse. I have grown used to her company and I believe I will miss it when she is gone. I do not admit this to her, however.

"Because you cannot see," I lie. A deep ache settles in the center of my chest as I study her. This feeling is unpleasant, uncomfortable, and I do not want to have it. I need space from her, for I believe she is somehow the cause.

I open my mouth, ready to give her an excuse so I may leave, but she interrupts my thoughts.

She shakes her head softly. "I can see just fine."

Turning my head to regard her, I reach out and brush a stray tendril of hair back from her face. I tuck it behind her ear as I study her blue eyes. "What do you mean?"

"There are more ways to see the world than just with your eyes."

I remember how she traced her hands over my face and body. "You are referring to touch?"

"That and other senses. For instance, you have a distinct scent."

"I did not know humans possessed such a keen sense of smell." I wonder if she finds my scent offensive or pleasing.

"You smell good. Like fresh rain and forest. And your face feels... regal." She grins.

I am oddly pleased that she likes my scent, but curious about her comment on my appearance. "How can you tell something like that?"

She lifts my hands to her cheeks, instructing me. "Close your eyes and use your sense of touch to learn the contours of my face."

I do as she instructs, marveling that she would allow me to touch her so intimately.

Her skin is petal-soft beneath my fingers. Cautiously, I trail my hands along her cheekbones and down to her jaw, following the elegant curve of her neck. The fluttering pulse of her artery quickens beneath my touch. I open my eyes to study her more closely, but do not tell her.

The soft mounds of her breasts peek just above the neckline of her dress, but I dare not move to touch them. I remember her initial fear that I would try to force-mate her. She trusts me now, and I feel oddly proud of this. I will not do anything she does not expressly permit.

I allow my hands to travel across her shoulders and then skim them lightly down her arms. Goosebumps pebble her flesh in their wake, and her breathing quickens.

When I reach her hands, I feel the small bones of her wrists and fingers. She truly is a delicate and lovely creature; charming in a way that I believed only the Fae or Elves could ever be.

To my surprise, she threads her fingers through mine and then smiles up at me. "You see? It is easy to learn someone simply by touch."

In this moment, I want her to see all of me. She explored me the day we first met but missed the parts that differ from a human. I was glad to conceal my monstrous form from her then, but now, I wish for her to know everything about me, just as I long instinctively to know everything about her.

"You missed some of my features when we first met," I tell her. "Would you like to study them now?"

"Yes. Very much so."

I drop to my knees before her so that she will have no

trouble reaching my face. Then I guide her hands to the top of my head.

Her small fingers brush lightly through my hair, skimming my scalp. She stills when she reaches my horns.

I worry she will be afraid because my features are unfamiliar, but instead, she smiles. "You have horns?"

"Yes."

She runs her hands over the small nubs on either side of my head beneath my dark hairline and then back down again.

"I have fangs, but I do not think it would be wise for you to touch those," I tease.

She laughs. "Good idea."

"I also have wings."

Her eyes widen. "Even in this form?"

"Yes. I am able to fly in this form as well."

"May I... may I touch them?" Her tone is hesitant.

"Yes. Step back, so I may turn."

She nods and I turn my back to her. "All right," I tell her.

She inhales sharply as soon as she touches my wings. I glance over my shoulder as her dainty fingers trace along the leathery folds and find a look of awestruck wonder on her face.

When she reaches the base where my wings attach to my back, I inhale sharply. My scales are sensitive here, but her touch feels incredible.

"You are beautiful," she whispers.

"Not exactly what a male wishes to hear from a female," I gently tease.

She laughs, stopping on a gasp. "What is that?"

I glance down, appalled to find that I have unconsciously wrapped my tail around her calf.

"It is my tail," I grimace, ashamed by my actions. Wrapping a tail around a female is a gesture of desire. If the female accepts this small touch, it is a sign that she is receptive to the mating ritual.

When she does not try to pull away, I swallow thickly as my stav presses insistently against the inside of my mating pouch, threatening to extend from my body. I should not be reacting this way to a human female. My kind do not mate hers.

She reaches around me to cup my cheek, coaxing me to turn and face her. "You've turned orange and pink."

I study my scales with a frown. "No, I am silver."

She laughs. "No. I mean your aura color. Orange means you're nervous, but the pink indicates that you are also happy."

For the first time in many years, this is the truth, but I do not understand why. Since she speaks so plainly to me, I decide to be truthful as well. I take her hand in mine. "Yes, I am."

Her cheeks flush a charming shade of pink as a stunning smile curves her lips. "I'm glad."

As we walk farther into the gardens, I gaze up at the many branches that hang down from the trees and a thought occurs to me. I turn to Alara. "Would a thin branch do for your walking cane?"

"As long as it is not heavy, it should work."

I gently squeeze her hand. "Wait here."

Extending my wings, I lift up into the trees. Finding a long, thin branch, I effortlessly snap it from the trunk and carry it back down to her. I place it in her hand. "What about this?"

Tipping her head to the side in a contemplative look, she runs her fingers up and down the branch, studying it. Then she bounces lightly on her toes. "This is perfect."

I observe as she tests it out, navigating the path beside me with only her cane to guide her. Such an ingenious idea. My human is very clever.

"Now that you are able to explore more easily, would you like to fly somewhere new?"

"Yes," she says, rewarding me with another dazzling smile.

I study her momentarily, admiring her fearlessness. This must be what attracts me to her. How is she so different from all the other humans? Each female that came before her cowered in fear or fell into despair upon accepting their fate. Yet, she smiles and happily spends time with me.

Me—a creature her kind consider a monster.

Even though our time is limited, I cannot help but be completely captivated by her spirit. I long to learn everything about this charming creature—my beguiling human female.

CHAPTER 10

ALARA

"Are you ready to go flying?" he asks.

"Yes."

In a whirl of dust and wind, he transforms. I reach out and run my hands along his scales, marveling at their silken feel. A puff of warm air parts my hair and I grin, knowing he is peering down at me.

"I can place you on my back if you'd like."

"I would," I tell him.

Something long and rope-like snakes around my waist, lifting me into the air. I hold tightly to the cord as my brow furrows.

"It is my tail," he explains.

"Oh," I reply as he places me on his back. I settle at the base of his neck and then lean forward slightly.

"Are you ready?" he asks.

Doubt creeps in. "You… you won't drop me, right?" I can think of nothing more terrifying than tumbling through darkness.

"I will not allow you to fall. I promise."

His words comfort me, and I relax. "All right. Then I'm ready."

With a sudden lurch, he lifts off. His muscles flex beneath me as he flaps his wings. After a moment, the roar of the ocean grows louder, and I smile when a spray of mist lands on my skin. We must be flying over the sea.

"The tide is high today," he calls out. "There is a large school of fish beneath the surface, their silver scales reflecting the sunlight like a glowing beacon. We are following along the coastline. There is a large rock outcropping up ahead where we will land at the edge of the water."

Even though I cannot see, the feel of the air rushing past me is invigorating. The first time I flew with him I was so afraid, and now I've never felt so alive.

I open my mouth to speak, but stop short as his muscles tense beneath me.

"What's wrong?"

"Do not be afraid," he says.

My chest tightens at his ominous words, but before I can ask any questions, he releases a deafening roar.

"Why did you do that?"

"Another Dragon is nearby. I am warning him not to cross into my territory. I would rather not battle another of my kind."

"Oh." I'm not really sure how to respond to that. Before I met Veron, I thought all Dragons were bad. Now, I'm beginning to wonder if many of them might be more like him.

He touches down so gently I do not even realize we've landed until he shifts into his two-legged form and grips my waist, lowering me to the ground. I reach back and feel his bare chest. A thought suddenly occurs to me, and I gasp. "You're naked?"

A booming laugh escapes him. "Yes. Clothing never

survives the shift intact. My Dragon body is so much larger than my two-legged form, they would simply shred when I transform. So, we do not normally bother with clothes."

I suppose that makes sense. Besides, it's not as if I can see anything scandalous anyway.

The dull roar of the ocean surrounds us. "What is this place? Where have you brought us?"

"It is my home the rest of the year. When I am in Dragon form, this is where I stay."

"Out in the open?" I ask, incredulous.

He laughs. "If the weather is nice, I do enjoy sleeping beneath the stars. But when it is not, I have a cave nearby."

I smile as I tease him. "Is it full of Dragon's treasure?"

"Of course. What kind of Dragon would I be if I did not sleep upon mountains of gold?"

I cannot tell if he is jesting or serious. I've heard Dragons sleep atop their treasure hoard, but I do not know of anyone who has personally seen such a thing and lived to tell the tale.

He continues. "That is why I must warn intruders away. I will not allow another to steal my treasure."

So… I suppose he wasn't joking then.

The cool ocean breeze caresses me, and I spread my arms wide as I tip up my chin, relishing the warmth of the sun upon my body. A small scrape of rocks beside me alerts me that Veron is standing close by.

"What are you doing?"

"Enjoying the sun on my skin." I smile, listening to the waves crashing against the shoreline below us. "This place must be beautiful," I whisper.

"I suppose it is," he muses.

I sit and hear him settle down beside me. I reach out, brushing my hands over the soft, thick grass that surrounds us. My fingers skim over a smooth surface and as I explore it further, I realize it is a small, flat stone. I turn it over in my palm and then place it in my pocket. I smile. "I think I'll keep this."

"It is only a stone," Veron replies. "Not a precious gem of any sort."

Of course, a Dragon would find no value in something so simple. I shrug. "I like the way it feels." I hold it out to him. "Besides, it's special because it is shaped like a heart."

"You are strange," he mumbles under his breath.

"But you like me, anyway." I grin as I tease him.

He sighs. "I suppose I do."

I blink owlishly, stunned by his admission. I thought he merely spent time with me because he was curious, as if I were some sort of specimen for him to observe. But now I smile, knowing that he enjoys my company as much as I enjoy his.

CHAPTER 11

VERON

As I sit beside her staring out at the sea, she laughs softly, and I find it is one of the most charming sounds I have ever heard.

"Would you believe me if I said that I used to have a fear of heights?"

I twist around to regard her. "How did you get over this fear?"

"By riding on the back of a Dragon."

I laugh. "You are very brave indeed. How is it that you are so fearless? What is your secret?"

She ducks her head. "When I first lost my sight, it was terrifying to always be in the dark."

My throat tightens, for I can only imagine how difficult it still must be for her.

"But I realized something, Veron."

I reach out and tuck a stray lock of hair behind her ear. "What was it?"

"I decided I could either live the rest of my life in fear or I could choose to embrace the blessings that remained. I'll admit there are still days that are hard. I miss my sight. Sunsets, flowers, trees… I wish I could see all the beautiful things I used to take for granted. But I make the choice each day to find something to be happy about and that conviction eases my fear."

I have never admired anyone as much as I do her at this moment. She is truly special, my brave human.

"I'm glad it was you, Veron."

I frown. "What do you mean?"

"I'm glad you were the Dragon." She smiles tentatively. "We have not known each other long, but I feel comfortable with you. Safe."

I lower my head. She does not know the truth about me. She does not know my dark secrets.

"Before I met you, I was terrified of Dragons. My grandfather used to tell us the story about the Dragon who burned the city of Bryndor."

My heart stutters and stops. I am the one of whom she speaks. I am the Dragon that rained down fire and destruction upon Bryndor. And all because I wanted the witch's treasure. "What did he tell you?" I ask, curious to know what she has heard.

"He said that Bryndor was once a shining city between the mountains and the sea. The castle used to be the most beautiful in all the kingdoms. It had shining, silver metal rooftops and gemstones encrusted all along the outer walls. My grandfather claimed that when the sun hit it just right, the entire structure glowed like a sparkling gem.

"Everyone knows the story of what happened there. My grandfather said it was demolition unlike anything he'd ever seen before. Almost nothing was left after the Dragon came through. The once magnificent city is now a mere shadow of its former glory. It is a terrible reminder of the destruction that can be wrought by Dragons."

I wince as I stare at the ground, unable to look at her as she speaks of what I did. I could have simply taken the treasure without leaving behind such devastation, but I cared not for the ruin and death I left behind. At the time, all I thought of was gold and gemstones. The lives of others did not matter to me.

She takes my hand, squeezing it gently. "I used to think all Dragons were bad because of that story, Veron. But now that I've met you, I know that isn't true." She smiles warmly. "You are a good man."

My heart constricts. She believes I am good, but I am not. She trusts me and I cannot bring myself to tell her the truth, for I do not want her to be afraid of me. "I am not a man. I am a Dragon," I gently remind her.

Her brow furrows softly. "Do you like being in your human form?"

I scoff. "I hardly appear human in my two-legged form. But part of the curse robs me of my ability to shift into this form during the rest of the year. Outside of the blood moon cycle, I am locked in my Dragon form and unable to think clearly. The witch somehow blocks me from my memories and my ability to reason. I suspect this is so I do not have more time to plan my revenge. Her curse reduces me to no more than a base animal. For the remainder of the year, I truly am a beast until the next blood moon rises."

"Oh," she says. "I am sorry. That must be terrible to... lose yourself like that."

I'm surprised that she apologizes for something that is not her fault. Humans are strange creatures indeed.

"So... normally when Dragons shift, they can think rationally?"

I frown. The answer to her question should be obvious;

my kind are incredibly intelligent. Why would she think we are reduced to mindless beasts while in Dragon form?

But considering Bryndor and all the destruction my kind rains down upon other kingdoms and cities... Especially when we covet their wealth—precious metals, gems, and such. We take what we want and care not of the ruin we leave behind.

"Yes," I tell her.

My heart squeezes painfully in my chest as I regard her. A terrible image of her being burned alive fills my mind and I shudder inwardly. I never cared about the lives of mere humans and yet, I cannot bear the thought of any harm coming to Alara.

* * *

WHEN WE RETURN to the castle, we have dinner on her balcony. Despite our conversation, my thoughts keep returning to her question about a Dragon's ability to think rationally. In all my long years, I have never once felt such regret as I do now. Especially when I think on how little regard I used to have for her kind.

My people consider hers inferior, but I have spent enough time with her to know this is not so. Humans may have fragile forms but Alara has shown me they are strong in other ways.

"Veron?" her soft voice rips me from my dark thoughts.

"Yes?"

"Is something wrong?"

"No," I lie and then wince inwardly when I remember she can sense when I am being untruthful.

She puts down her fork and leans forward, sweeping her hand across the table as if searching for mine. I move my hand toward her and as soon as she finds it, she entwines our fingers. "You can tell me, Veron. Whatever it is. We promised to be truthful with each other, remember?"

"I do not wish to speak of it."

"Why?"

"I do not have to explain myself to you," I reply, my voice coming out a bit harsher than I'd intended.

She retracts her hand as if burned. "Fine," she murmurs, the hurt easily read in her features.

I hate that my words have upset her. I clench my jaw in frustration. Why does Alara affect me like this? I should not care about the emotions of a human. Running my hand roughly through my hair, I stand from the table.

"Where are you going?"

Anywhere but here. I cannot bear to be around her any longer. Not when she causes me to feel like this. In the center of my chest is a terrible ache so painful, I want to claw it from my body just to be rid of it. "To hunt."

Before she can say anything else, I shift forms and leap from the balcony. I extend my wings and glide out over the sea before making a long, slow arc back toward the castle and then into the woods. Scanning the forest, I search for prey, giving myself over to the dark instincts of the hunt.

CHAPTER 12

ALARA

I listen as Veron leaves. The dull roar of the sea quickly drowns out the loud flapping of his wings as he sails off the balcony. I don't understand why he is so annoyed right now. His color shifted from the gray of sadness to the light red of agitation the moment I asked him what was wrong.

Sighing heavily, I decide to go downstairs and out to the gardens. I can still feel the warmth of the sun on my skin, telling me I have a bit of time before it gets dark. Veron and I often walk the garden paths after dinner, but I suppose I will have to go by myself this evening.

As I reach for my walking cane, I recall how Veron retrieved another branch for me just the other night during our walk, so I'd have a spare.

With a heavy sigh, I carefully navigate down the stairs and to the gardens beyond the courtyard. The soft gravel of the pathway crunches under my shoes as I walk among the flowering plants. My thoughts turn to my sister. I hope she is doing well. I miss her terribly.

I recall walking arm in arm with her through the flowering fields near the edge of our village every year during the Spring Festival. Last year, Garen surprised her with a bouquet of roses. It is a tradition for a man to present flowers to the woman he has pledged himself to.

Each year since they were fifteen, Garen has brought Lilly flowers. They have loved each other for so long and have been planning their marriage for the past three years. I have always been happy for them, but envious as well. I've never had a love of my own. Absently, I palm the heart-shaped stone in my pocket as my thoughts turn to Veron.

I shake my head softly. I'm falling in love with him, and I don't care that he's a Dragon. He's kind and caring and thoughtful in a way that I never imagined he could be. We spend hours talking about everything and nothing. I enjoy spending time with him, and I value his friendship. But lately, I've been wanting more.

Knowing that my time here is so short makes my longing all the worse. Is it wrong to want a small taste of happiness and love before I fade away into nothing?

Veron told me that Dragons are incapable of love, so I know I cannot hope for him to return my feelings. It is not his fault; it is simply his nature. Besides, it is enough just to spend time in his presence, and I would not trade these moments for anything.

"Alara!" a familiar voice calls out, startling me.

I pause, wondering if I'm hearing things.

"Alara!" My head whips toward the voice. "Help me!" My heart stops when I realize it is my sister, calling to me from the direction of the forest.

"Lilly!" I cry out. "Where are you?"

"Alara, help me!"

The raw fear in her tone makes me panic. Sweeping my walking cane back and forth before me, I race as fast as I can toward the sound of her voice. "Lilly!"

She calls out again, but she sounds much farther away than before. My cane hits something hard. I sweep my hand out and it slaps against the trunk of a large tree. I must be at the edge of the woods. But why is my sister here?

"Lilly, where are you?"

"Help me!"

I don't have time to wonder. My sister is in some sort of trouble. Using my cane with one hand, I wave my other arm back and forth in front of me to avoid hitting any branches. It's frustrating, because it makes my progress that much slower, but I cannot give up. My sister needs me.

Something whooshes past me, above the tree line. A strong gust of wind wraps around my form, whipping through my hair and billowing my dress around my ankles. I tip my head up toward the sky, listening intently for any other noise. When I hear it again, I call out, "Veron? Is that you?"

A thunderous roar answers, and ice fills my veins as I recognize the sound. It is a Dragon in the forest, but I'm certain it's not Veron, just as surely as I know I am being hunted.

Fear twists deep in my gut. If I remain still, I am dead. But if I move, I might only be rushing toward my demise. My heart hammers as I weigh my options. I'd rather try and take my chances, than stay here and wait to die. "Veron!" I cry out and then break into a run.

CHAPTER 13

VERON

Flying along the edge of the woods, a familiar scent drifts on the wind. My nostrils flare and I realize it is the Dragon I detected near my territory several days ago. It seems he has returned, undeterred by my show of aggression.

I spiral up toward the dark clouds above the tree line. From here, I can see the castle. I glance back at Alara's balcony and the softly glowing light from her window. An image of her burning alive fills my mind, and I close my eyes as I struggle to push down this dark and terrible thought.

It will not do to have another Dragon nearby, for he could be a danger to her. Furiously, I flap my wings as I race toward the intruder. He will pay for invading my territory.

I follow his scent deep into the forest, but no matter how strong it gets, I cannot seem to locate him. My thoughts return to Alara. Is he here to take her from me?

Surely not. He would have no interest in her as a mate, but that does not mean he won't kill her. I must find this other Dragon and chase him from my territory. I will not allow a threat to my human to remain so close to my home.

My human. Even as this possessive thought fills my mind, I realize I cannot allow myself to become so attached to Alara. I cannot claim her as mine. She will be gone… turned to stone like all the rest when the last petal falls from the rosebush. But how can I distance myself from her when she has asked me to spend time with her?

I curse in frustration as I push the dark thoughts of her impending death aside. I circle back to the castle and fly straight to her balcony. A terrible weight settles deep in my chest as I think of any harm coming to her. I need to see her—my mind demanding proof that she is alright. I knock on the door, but she does not answer.

"Alara?" I call out, but everything is silent.

I pull the balcony door open and step inside her room. As soon as I do, I notice the door to the hallway is ajar, telling me she is not here. I race through it and down the hall to the first floor, calling out to her.

I step outside into the front courtyard and close my eyes as I focus on her scent. The delicate bouquet of her distinct scent still lingers in the air, telling me she was here not long ago. I follow her fragrance deep into the woods beyond the castle.

It is darker here beneath the thick canopy of trees and my senses become heightened in response. My eyes adjust quickly to the darkness and my ears pick up the sounds of several creatures scurrying to retreat as I draw closer. Even in my two-legged form, they know what I am, and they are right to fear a superior predator.

A cool breeze runs through the woods. I stop abruptly and my nostrils flare. Carried on the wind, I detect the scent of the other Dragon. The forest is eerily silent and still, and I realize that I am not the only one to pick up this scent.

I thought he had moved on since I was unable to locate him, but it seems I was wrong.

My every nerve is humming in acute awareness and anticipation as I track him into the woods. My heart pounds and blood flows through my veins like liquid fire. Murderous thoughts consume me. How dare this intruder come into my territory.

My thoughts turn to Alara. She is here somewhere too, and I must find her before the other Dragon does.

Alara's scent becomes stronger, and I know she is close.

A booming roar ricochets through the forest, followed by Alara's panicked cry as she calls out my name. "Veron!"

Instantly, I shift into my Dragon form and tear through the trees toward the sound of her voice, desperate to find her. In the distance, I see the form of my rival. His red scales catch the moonlight as he races through the forest. His massive wings billow out like great sails as he chases her, hunting her as if she were an animal instead of a sentient being.

Long, icy tendrils of fear pierce my spine; images of sharp claws and teeth ripping through her flesh fill my mind. Primitive instincts surge through me as I bellow a challenge.

He ignores me. My heart pounds and anger burns through my body like fire, stripping away all control, leaving nothing but base and primal rage in its wake. My claws extend as the urge to protect what is mine consumes me.

How dare he hunt her for his amusement.

A flash of movement catches my eye and I see Alara running up ahead. The acrid scent of her fear taints the air as she calls out to me again. "Veron!"

She can hear the red Dragon as he chases her through the woods, but she cannot see the death that comes for her. Fire races up my throat and my muscles burn with effort as I come up even beside my rival. I will die before I let him touch her.

I dip my wing and slam into his side. We tumble through the air in a tangled mass of teeth and claws, downing several trees as we tear into each other. A vicious and primal thing uncoils from deep within me as I fight this intruder who dared invade my territory.

"You would fight me over a human?" he grinds out as I wrestle him to the ground.

"She is mine!"

Blinding pain rips through me as his sharp claws rake across my side. He struggles, writhing beneath me as I pin him to the forest floor. But he cannot escape my iron embrace, and I have no intention of letting him go. He dared to hunt Alara and now… I will be certain that he hunts no more.

I clamp my jaws around his neck and rip out his throat. Obsidian blood sprays the woods around us, covering my scales in the thick, viscous fluid. I watch with cold satisfaction as the light fades from his yellow eyes.

Once I am certain he is dead, I shift back into my two-legged form and rush to Alara. Joy, brighter than a thousand stars, fills my mind as soon as I see her and know that she is unharmed.

"Alara," I pant out her name as I drop to my knees before her.

Her eyes are wide and her hair in disarray as her hands pat over my body, smearing the blood across my scales. "Veron, you're hurt."

"I will heal."

Despite the gore that covers me, she wraps her arms around me and buries her face in my chest. "Thank the gods you're all right," she whispers. "What happened to the other Dragon? Is he gone?"

I raise my hand and gently place it on her head. As I run my fingers over the long, silken strands, a long exhale escapes me. I am relieved she is unharmed. I place two fingers under her chin, tipping her face up to me. "I killed him. Why were you out here?"

"I—I thought I heard my sister's voice, calling out to me from deep in the woods."

I grit my teeth. A trick—something to lure her into the forest and into danger. I lift my head and scan the area around us. To my astonishment, the red Dragon's body shimmers and then fades away into nothing.

A flicker of light catches my eye in the distance. I whip my head toward it and see the blood witch. Her lips curl up in an evil grin as she fades into the darkness.

Looking down at myself, I realize the marks on my body from the battle are still there, along with the blood. What kind of sorcery is this? Why did the witch lure Alara? Was my fight with the Dragon a test of some sort?

I cup Alara's cheek. "The voice you heard was not your sister. You were lured here. It was a trap, and I believe the blood witch who cursed me set it."

"Why would she do this?"

I'm troubled because I do not have an answer to this question. "I do not know."

Tears fill her eyes. "I'm sorry I went into the woods, Veron. I just… when I heard my sister's voice, I had to go."

"Why are you crying?" I ask, unable to hide my distress. "I thought you were not hurt."

"I'm not hurt. I'm just happy you're alive."

I reach up and gently wipe at the moisture on her cheek. Rubbing the clear liquid between my thumb and forefinger, I study it before looking back at her in confusion. "Humans cry when they are happy?"

A soft puff of air escapes her lips as she smiles. "Yes, we do."

Her hands travel over my form. She inhales sharply as her fingers encounter my many wounds. "Are you in pain, Veron?"

"I will be fine." I stand and wince, but hide my discomfort so I do not distress her. "I will heal. It will just take a bit of time."

And I would. My kind heal rather quickly compared to many of the other races.

I cup Alara's chin and tilt her head up to me. "Promise me you will not leave the castle without my knowing ever again."

"I promise."

When we return to the castle, I am hesitant to let her leave my sight. Dragons do not love and yet… when I knew the red Dragon wanted to kill her, strangling tendrils of fear took root deep within me. They are rooted there still, and worry consumes me, knowing that she who is most precious could have been killed—taken from me in an instant.

My gaze tracks Alara as she returns to her room. Is this what the blood witch wanted me to understand? Is this the emotion she wanted to instill in me? A fear greater than any I have ever known before? Is this the love that she spoke of that she wanted me to learn?

It cannot be. Dragons do not love.

CHAPTER 14

ALARA

Veron has been almost constantly by my side since the day he saved me in the woods. We have been together a total of fifteen days. As we sit on the cliff near his Dragon cave, I lean against him, enjoying the sounds of the waves crashing along the shoreline below.

A soft, lilting song drifts up from the sea and I turn my head slightly to listen. "Do you hear that?"

"It is the merfolk," Veron grumbles.

"It's beautiful."

He growls low. "If you at any time feel compelled to walk into the sea, warn me first."

"What?"

He touches my cheek, turning my face toward him. "You do not feel a call to the ocean when you hear their song?"

"No."

"Hmmm." He trails off as if contemplating my answer.

A loud crack of thunder overhead startles me. I only have

a moment to recover before cold and heavy rain pours down, pelting the earth all around us.

"Quickly!" Veron pulls me up beside him. "We must take shelter."

Something sharp digs into the skin on the back of my hand as he drags me behind him, and I realize it must be his claws. I ignore the sharp pain as we race toward shelter.

The rain suddenly stops. We must have found cover because I can still hear it pounding the ground behind me. The air is thick and smells of damp earth. Shivering, I reach out my hand and touch a rough stone surface. "Where are we?"

My voice echoes loudly, telling me we are in an expansive yet enclosed space. Small rocks scrape beneath my shoes as I step forward. "Is this your cave or a different one?"

"It is mine. All of the others nearby are too small for us to be safe in." Booming thunder rolls across the sky. "We must stay here until the storm passes. It is cold, but we are fortunate it is only rain and not snow outside. Even so, it would not be safe for me to fly you back to the castle in this weather. Your kind are fragile and prone to getting sick."

A smile tugs at my lips as I begin wringing the hem of my drenched skirt. "You make us sound as if we are made of glass."

"Is it not the truth?" he asks. "Compared to a Dragon, you have no natural defenses. No claws, fangs, or wings. And your flesh is petal-soft compared to our scales."

He's right that humans do not have all those things. But just because we are not fire-breathing Dragons doesn't mean we're weak.

He continues, "And yet, you are brave."

His words fill me with pride and a strange warmth. Despite my chattering teeth, I reply, "Thank you."

"I did not know humans could possess such courage. It is… surprising," he adds.

I grin. "And I didn't know Dragons could be capable of kindness."

He guides me to a nearby rock to sit down and takes a seat beside me. My outer robe is soaked through and I shiver as the cold air hits my skin.

"You must remove your wet clothing or else you may fall ill."

In any other situation, I would protest and stubbornly remain in my wet clothes. But my time is already limited. What does it matter if he sees me with barely anything on? We are alone and it is not as if he could tell another human.

"All right," I stand and take off my robe, and then begin to remove my dress.

He makes a strangled sound in the back of his throat, and I stop. "What is wrong?"

"You—you mean to undress completely?" He stumbles over his words.

My cheeks heat in embarrassment as my self-consciousness returns. "I… I don't want to catch cold and… it's not as if anyone else will see me. I would not be so forward otherwise, but I'm not ready to—" My voice catches, unable to form the rest of my sentence. *I'm not ready to die just yet.* Especially not from catching a cold because I insisted on preserving my modesty.

"I understand," he assures me, his color turning a deep shade of gray.

"Are you sad for me?" I ask, wondering at his aura color.

"I pity you."

"I don't need your pity. Yours or anyone else's. Despite my lack of sight, I am perfectly capable of taking care of myself."

He takes my hand. "I do not judge you for your blindness. I meant that I pity your short lifespan because of the curse."

I gently squeeze his hand. "Thank you. I'm sorry you have to suffer as well."

He stills, falling silent. Finally, he releases my hand to let me finish undressing.

I remove my dress, leaving only the band around my breasts and the small slip of fabric that covers my pelvis and backside. Not modest by any means, but such concerns no longer matter.

He takes my clothes. "Hopefully, these will dry while we wait. I will make us a fire."

I start to ask how he plans to do such a thing, but then remember that he is a Dragon. If anyone can make a fire, it would be him. Soon enough, the sound of crackling flames suffuses the cavern. I stretch my hands out toward the warmth.

He inhales sharply and then his hand wraps around my wrist, pulling it toward him. "Your hand. What happened?" he asks, worry evident in his tone.

I try to pull it away from him, but he does not let go.

"Was this from me? My claws when I—"

"It's fine, Veron. I know you did not mean to hurt me."

"Forgive me, Alara. I forgot to retract them. Your skin is too soft. It offers your kind almost no protection."

I huff out a frustrated breath. "I'm tired of hearing about how weak and fragile you think we humans are, all right? I'm fine."

"But it is true. Compared to Dragons, humans are—"

"No, it's not," I snap.

I'm surprised when he sits next to me and wraps an arm around my side to tug me close. "Forgive me, Alara," he murmurs. "You are right. Before I met you, I had no idea human females could be as fierce or as brave as Dragons."

I release a small sigh of contentment as his warmth seeps into my skin. When he wraps his wings around me as well, I snuggle against him. The heat is pure bliss. "Thank you, Veron. You see?" I tease. "I am always right."

He barks a laugh and hugs me even tighter. "So it seems."

I nestle against him. Sometimes, I think it's strange how comfortable I am with him, despite having known him for such a short amount of time.

As we sit together in his cave, I listen to the raging storm outside and the sound of the waves crashing along the cliff wall. I imagine Veron sleeping here in his Dragon form all alone.

"What is it like, living here?" I ask. "Are you lonely?"

"My people tend to live solitary lives until we find a mate. We barely even interact with each other. I have grown used to the solitude," he replies, though I note a hint of sadness in his voice.

I shake my head. "No, you haven't."

He stiffens beside me.

"I can sense your color, remember? And right now, it is gray because you are sad." I take his hand and entwine our fingers. "You are the last person I will spend time with on this earth. Let us speak openly to one another."

"Fine," he murmurs. "If we are being truthful… I wish I had not brought you to my cave."

"Why?"

"Because when you are gone, I will remember being here with you."

"But I thought you lost your memories when locked in your Dragon form the rest of the year."

He sighs heavily, his gray color turning even darker to match his growing sadness. "You, I believe I will remember, regardless of the curse."

I'm surprised by his admission. "Does that mean that you'll miss me when I'm gone?"

He tightens his wings around me. "I do not understand why, but I feel oddly protective of you—possessive, even. Though the urge is unnatural, I cannot deny that it is there. So yes, I will miss you when you are… gone, Alara."

"This was my choice. You don't have to mourn me. I chose to come in my sister's stead. You cannot blame yourself for that."

"Yes, I can," he says grimly. "If I had only known what would happen, I never would have tried to steal from the witch."

"I'm sorry she cursed you, Veron," I whisper, tracing my hand up his arm to cup his cheek. "But the blood witch is to blame. Not you. She is the one who involved innocent people when she cast the curse upon you." Moisture touches my skin and I realize it is a tear. I did not think that Dragons could cry.

He places his hand over mine and leans into my palm as if relishing my touch. "I wish that were true, Alara. But I am just as much to blame as she is."

I don't understand why he carries such guilt. It was only treasure, and he is a Dragon. It's not as if he got away with it. She caught him. "Why do you blame yourself?"

He drops his forehead gently to mine. "Please," he whispers. "Let us not speak of it further."

Reluctantly, I nod. He's hiding something from me, but I don't want to press him. He'll tell me when he is ready.

We sit before the fire, holding each other. I continue to run my hands up and down his arms, chest, and face. It's as if I cannot stop touching him—and the truth is, I don't want to. It feels good to be connected to someone. He must feel the same because he does not stop touching me either.

This is not about desire. It is more as if we are exploring

one another and marveling at both our connection and our differences, enjoying this closeness that exists between us.

I have heard that shared trauma can bond two people very quickly and I suppose sharing this curse could have the same effect.

"When I was little," I whisper. "I was so afraid of storms I would crawl into bed with my sister. She would hold me and sometimes even sing to calm me down."

"How did you overcome your fear?"

I laugh softly as the memory returns. "It was shortly after I lost my sight. A strong storm came through and I made my way to her room. I wondered why she was so hesitant to allow me into her bed, but I didn't question her. After all, I was fifteen—old enough that I shouldn't have still feared the thunder."

"What happened?" Curiosity laces his tone.

"As soon as I lay down, I heard a strange noise—a scrape against the floor. Quiet footsteps. I did not want to alarm my sister or alert the intruder that I knew he was there. So, I grabbed the candlestick off the bedside table and jumped out of bed, rushing in the sound's direction to attack."

He gasps. "Who was it?"

I chuckle. "It was Garen, her fiancé. They feared being discovered in bed together—even though they were only sleeping—since a woman under the age of twenty-five may not lie with a man. They worried I would accidentally reveal their secret."

"Why is that?"

"All women must remain maidens in case they are chosen as the sacrifice to the Dragon."

He scoffs. "What? Who ordered such a thing? That is not part of the curse."

"It isn't?"

"No," he denies vehemently. "How ridiculous. I am a

Dragon. Why would I ever want to mate a human, maiden or not?" He stills suddenly, tipping my chin up as if studying me. "How old are you?"

"Twenty-three."

"Does that mean you have never…"

My cheeks heat. "No one wants a blind girl in my village. I had no one besides my sister. She loves Garen, and I wished them happiness, a family and children… all the joys I knew I'd never experience."

He tugs me into his chest in an oddly soothing gesture. "I am sorry… even if you insist it is not my fault."

"I'm not sorry, Veron, not now that I've met you. After all," I tease, "how many people can say that they've ridden a Dragon?"

He laughs. "We can fly every day, if you like. The curse binds me so that I must always return to the castle or the area around my cave each night. And I cannot go beyond the borders of the forest, for I couldn't risk shifting back to human form. Someone might see me and turn to stone. But there are still many places we may visit."

I sigh and rest my head on his shoulder. "That sounds lovely." A thought occurs to me. "Why do you care if any other humans turn to stone?"

"Truthfully, I do not know. I only understand that the mere thought of causing another to suffer such a fate leaves me feeling… uncomfortable. As if there is a great knot in my stomach."

"That's called guilt," I tell him. "Remorse."

"Strange," he mumbles, so low I almost miss it.

Indeed, it is. My Dragon is learning to feel.

CHAPTER 15

VERON

I awaken with a start. The fog of my nightmares recedes; dark images retreat like tides from the shore. My heart pounds in my chest and I pull Alara close, glad that she is unharmed and we are safe in my cave.

Lately, I have been plagued by terrible dreams of someone coming to take her from me. The nightmare always ends with her dying before I can save her. The fear these dreams instill in me is so great, I often fly to her window once I awaken just to be sure she is safe.

The storm has finally moved on. She is still asleep. I wrap my arms and wings tightly around her. I have never been this close to another, but I find I do not mind it. It lets me study her closely. She is a delicate and charming creature, my human, and I am completely captivated. I would do anything to keep her here with me and save her from the curse.

Dragon females are strong and fierce. Many of them are even twice the size of the males. Alara's form is soft and fragile, but it belies a strength of will that is as strong as any of my kind. She took the place of her sister, even knowing the sentence was death, and I stare down at her in wonder. I never knew humans possessed such courage.

It is strange that the merfolk's song did not affect her. I worried for a moment that I'd have to hold her captive in my arms to keep her from walking to the sea and into the arms of those troublesome fish. I have heard the only ones who are immune to their siren call are Dragons and those who are in love. Could it be that Alara loves me?

The firelight casts a warm glow throughout the cave as it reflects off my many piles of gold and precious gems. It took me several long years to acquire this wealth, but as I look at Alara, I realize that I would give up all of it for her.

She has asked me many times about the curse, but I cannot find the strength to admit my sins. I may not have stolen the witch's treasure, but I realize now that what I took from her was far more valuable than any amount of bullion or jewels.

I killed her mate when I burned my way through the castle and for the first time, as I look at Alara asleep in my arms, I understand why the witch cursed me.

Dragons do not love. I have always believed that such emotion was irrelevant and meaningless, but I know now that I was wrong. My people care only for gold and gems, but holding her in my arms, I understand the truth. Alara is more dear than any of those things—she is my greatest treasure. I did not intend to become so close to a human, but I cannot undo what is already done.

As if my deep thoughts have somehow disturbed her, Alara stirs softly in my arms and nestles closer to my chest. I am loath to wake her, for I do not wish to let her go. She lifts her head and tilts her ear toward the cave entrance. "Is the storm over?"

"Yes."

"Should we return to the castle?"

I am reluctant to leave, but I know her bed is far more comfortable for her than the ground. "If you wish."

She smiles up at me as she places her hand on my chest. "I don't want to impose any longer on you. I'm sure you're probably not comfortable."

To be honest, it is no bother as I find that I enjoy holding her like this, but I do not admit it.

By the time we return, it is already dark. After circling the castle, I alight on the balcony outside her room. I bid her goodnight as she walks in through the door, shutting it softly behind her.

I scrape my hands over my face as frustration burns through me. Alara can never be mine. She would not want me if she knew the truth—that I am the Dragon that burned the city of Bryndor to ash. I must make certain that she never finds out.

Even if she cannot be mine, I must find a way to save Alara from the curse. I cannot bear the notion of her turning to stone like the others. It will break me.

CHAPTER 16

VERON

It has been twenty-two days we have been together, her and I. Time has gone by much too fast since she first arrived, and I can hardly bear to think on the fate that awaits her. I have tried several times to summon the blood witch, wanting to beg her to spare Alara's life, but to no avail. The witch has not come to me.

As I sit across from Alara in the gardens, I study her intently. Something is different about her today, but I am uncertain what it is. I cock my head. "You are hiding something. What is it?"

She grins and I realize I am right. "How did you know?"

I narrow my eyes. "I have studied you for days. I know all of your… tells."

She laughs. "Is that so?"

"Yes."

"Well, if you must know… I have a surprise for you."

Curious, I ask, "What is it?"

"Close your eyes."

I frown. "Why?"

"Just do it."

Reluctantly, I close my eyes, although I realize she would probably never know if I kept them open.

"Are they closed?"

"Yes," I reply, and it is the truth. I do not wish to lie to her, so I close my eyes and wait patiently to see what she will do.

Her warm hands trace up my arm toward my neck and then I hear the soft rustle of her clothing as she moves behind me. A small weight settles on my chest just below my throat, and then I feel a soft cord against the scales of my neck.

"Open your eyes."

I open them and look down at my chest, discovering the heart-shaped stone she found on the cliffs outside my cave. She has turned it into a necklace. I take her hand and then face her. "This is yours. Why have you given this to me?"

"Because I wanted you to have it." She smiles. "Something to remember me by when I'm gone."

My heart clenches as I look down at her. Unable to stop myself, I pull her to my chest, wrapping my arms and wings tightly around her.

She pulls back and cups my cheek. "Don't be sad, Veron."

"How can I not be? Soon you will—"

She presses her finger to my lips to silence me. "*Shhh*. Let's not talk of what we cannot change and instead enjoy each other's company." She smiles warmly. "All right, my Dragon?"

I arch a brow. "Your... Dragon?"

"Yes," she chuckles, and a teasing smile plays across her lips. "While I am here, you are mine."

Emotions lodge in my throat, and I recognize them now for what they are. My kind are not supposed to feel such things and yet... I do. I can hardly speak around them.

I place my hand over hers on my face, staring down at she who is more precious than any gold or gems. Alara is my greatest treasure and I belong to her: body, mind, heart, and soul.

Gently, I drop my forehead to her own and close my eyes as I breathe out the words. "I am yours."

As I hold her close, I wish we could remain this way always. These mere few weeks have felt like an eternity, as if I have known her forever. Each day, we fly somewhere new. I would never have imagined she had a fear of heights, considering how eagerly she anticipates our flights each morning.

She trusts me not to let her fall, and I am in awe of her strength of spirit. Dragons are fearless because of our superior forms: thick scales impervious to regular arrows or swords, sharp and deadly talons and fangs, and the ability to breathe fire down upon our enemies. Humans do not have any of these assets, yet Alara is as fierce as she is brave.

A smile tugs at my lips as I recall when she stood up to me, demanding that I apologize to her for my anger. A human demanding an apology from a Dragon. I shake my head softly. Who else would dare such a thing but her?

She takes my hand and leads me farther into the gardens. She loves the eternal spring that the enchantment maintains. We have now come here so often, she is the one leading me along the path to the waterfall. We pass the enchanted rosebush on our way and my chest tightens. The blooms are not quite as full as they once were. Our time will end soon, and I can hardly bear knowing that she will turn to stone like all the others.

A warm hand travels up my arm to cup my cheek. "Don't be sad, Veron. Today is a good day. We're going swimming."

I cannot help the smile that tugs at my lips in response. "We are?"

"Yes. It is on our list of things to do while I am here. Remember?"

I nod. That conversation feels as if it happened so very long ago. "Yes, I do."

She takes off her dress, leaving her in nothing but her undergarments. She is not shy around me ever since that day in the cave because she knows I would never harm or take advantage of her.

She holds out her hand, and I step forward and take it. "Ready?" She grins.

"In a moment. I must first make a sweep of the castle grounds."

"Why?" Her eyebrows draw together.

I do not wish to admit that she rouses my protective instincts as if she were my mate. Even knowing how short our time together is, I cannot deny that I want her to be mine. But I know this cannot be. She is fragile and I fear I could hurt her if we were to mate. Besides, I doubt she would want me. Especially if she knew the truth of my sins.

Nightmares continue to plague my sleep. I dream of fire and flame engulfing her and wake up panting in fear, not for myself, but for her. So, I have taken to frequently checking the castle perimeter for intruders. I do not doubt I could defend us against any invaders, but my dreams leave me with an edge of worry.

"I will return soon," I assure her.

"Alright. Hurry back." She smiles and my heart fills with warmth because I know that lovely smile is meant for me.

"I will."

I fly in a tight loop around the castle grounds and find nothing amiss. Satisfied we are alone, I fly back to the gardens. I glance at the pool beneath the waterfall and my stomach drops when I notice her body floating motionless on the surface. Shifting into my human form, I dive into the water.

"Alara!" I cry out as I swim toward her. "Alara!"

Relief floods my system when she lifts her head. "Veron? What's wrong?"

I rush toward her and gather her in my arms, wrapping my wings tightly around her. "I saw you floating, and I thought—" The words catch in my throat, and I swallow hard against the emotions welling up inside me.

She strokes my cheek. "I'm fine, my Dragon. You don't have to worry about me. I've been swimming since I was a child."

I can hardly focus on her words. The image of her floating so still upon the water fills my mind and I cannot stop touching her. I smooth my hand up and down her back to reassure myself that she is well.

She shivers slightly. "Is the water not warm enough for you?" I ask, concerned.

"No, I'm fine."

Her cheeks are flushed a deep-red hue. I know my body temperature is slightly warmer than hers, so perhaps holding her so closely is causing her to overheat. I allow my wings to drop to my sides and take her hand instead.

We swim together and I gently guide her to the back of the waterfall, passing under the overhang. "We are behind the falls," I tell her, describing what I see. "The water is like a curtain, hiding us from the rest of the world."

She pulls herself closer to me. Brushing her hand up my arm, she touches my face and then smiles. "Thank you, Veron."

"For what?"

"For always taking the time to describe the world to me. I appreciate it more than you know."

I want to promise that I will always be her eyes, but

emotions constrict my throat again and I cannot speak. Besides, my words would be a lie; she will not live for much longer.

"Do not despair, my Dragon," she murmurs. "I can see your aura."

"I'm sorry," I whisper. "But I cannot bear it."

"Bear what?"

I drop my chin to my chest and close my eyes against the pain. "Knowing that you will—" I stop just short of saying it.

"Try not to think of it, Veron."

A deep ache settles in my chest. "How can I not?"

"You've been through this many times, my Dragon. You will survive, just as you have before. Soon, you will forget about me."

"Do not say such things," I snap. "You do not understand. You are the first, the only one I have ever—" I swallow back a sob as I crush her to my chest. "Your people consider me a monster, and yet you are not afraid to touch me."

She shakes her head gently, whispering, "You are not a monster. You are a Dragon. You are *my* Dragon, Veron."

I tuck a loose lock of hair behind her ear as I study her features, memorizing the contours of her lovely face. I run my fingers lightly across her cheek. She is more precious and beautiful than all the gold and gems in the world.

She cups my face and I lean into her palm, relishing the feel of her soft, warm skin against my own.

"Dragons do not love," I whisper softly. "I did not love before you. *You* awakened this in me—this part of me that loves." I rest my forehead on hers. "My people have long lives, and I will love you until I draw my last breath, Alara. I cannot bear the thought of losing you."

A beautiful smile lights her face as she reaches up to skim her fingers over my ridged brow. "You love me, Veron? You truly love me, my Dragon?"

I turn my face into her hand and press a tender kiss to her palm. "Yes," I murmur. "With all that I am."

She runs the soft pad of her thumb across my bottom lip, and I am transfixed as she leans in to gently press her mouth to mine. Her lips are soft and warmer than I imagined.

She opens her mouth, and my tongue finds hers. She moans and then twines her arms around my neck, holding me close as we explore each other. At first, our kiss is slow as her smooth tongue strokes against mine, but it quickly turns into something more. I wrap my arms and wings around her, pressing her back against the wall.

I groan as she wraps her legs around my waist and rolls her hips against mine. My stav lengthens and extends from my mating pouch, seeking the warmth of her center. Only the thin barrier of the small scrap of fabric between her thighs separates us. It is the most exquisite torture; I long to join my body to hers.

A cool night breeze billows from the ocean and she shivers against me.

This will not do. "Let us go back inside," I murmur. "It is too cold for you here."

She nods and I carry her out of the water and back to the castle. I dry us both and then bring her to the bed. Gently, I lay her beneath the covers and then move to the fireplace and start a fire to warm her.

She is silent as I work, and I worry that perhaps she has decided she does not want me. She did not return my confession. She did not tell me that she loved me.

When I am finished, I move back to the bed. She reaches her hand toward me, and I take it. She entwines our fingers and pulls me beneath the covers with her, turning to me and lightly touching my cheek. "Your color is orange, Veron. Why are you worried?"

She has always asked for honesty, so I withhold nothing. "I have told you how I feel, but you have not told me—"

Her finger goes to my lips, silencing me. She smiles. "I love you too, Veron. With all my heart."

Although she has confessed, I must ask again to be sure. "You are certain you want me?"

She nods as a pink bloom spreads across her cheeks. Tentatively, she bites her lower lip. "Will you hold me?"

"Yes."

I fold my arms and wings around her tightly. She tenses at first, clearly nervous. After a moment, she relaxes against me.

I gently nuzzle her hair. "We do not have to do anything you do not wish, Alara."

She trails her hand up my arm to stroke my shoulder. "I'm sorry, Veron... I've never done this before and I'm a bit nervous."

I carefully run my fingers through her long, silken hair. "It is enough to simply hold you," I whisper. "I want only to give you pleasure, Alara." My fingers drift across her cheek, and a warm blush trails across her skin in their wake. "We cannot fully mate, my beloved. I am much stronger than you; I worry I might hurt you."

Her breath tickles my cheek. "You won't hurt me, Veron. I trust you. Completely."

I clench my jaw as need burns through me like fire. I long to claim her as mine, but I cannot. "You do not understand, Alara."

"Then, tell me, Veron. How does a Dragon claim his mate?"

"If you were a female Dragon, I would present myself to you in my two-legged form and then challenge you to the mating battle. If I conquered you, I would sink my fangs into your neck to mark you as mine, holding you in place as I filled you with my seed."

As I gaze upon her naked form, I realize that my beautiful Alara should be worshipped, not conquered. Her petal-soft skin flushes a lovely shade of pink with arousal. When I place a tender kiss to the curve of her neck and shoulder, her heart rate quickens and the scent of her need grows even stronger, driving me mad with desire.

"If we cannot fully mate, can I at least touch you?" she whispers.

I want her so much, I'm on the razor's edge of my control. Despite my better judgment, I can think of nothing I want more. "Yes."

She brushes her fingers along the planes of my chest and abdomen, tracing my body as if memorizing me through touch. Her hand travels lower and when she reaches my mating pouch, my stav is already fully extended from my body and painfully engorged.

CHAPTER 17

ALARA

I wrap my hand around his manhood and am surprised that he is so large, my fingers do not touch. Ridges cover his entire length, and my thighs squeeze together involuntarily at the thought of what that might feel like inside me.

"My stav," he groans. "It is very sensitive." He places his hand over mine. "You do not have to—"

"I want to touch you, Veron," I say softly.

He growls low in his throat as I run my thumb over the tip, catching a bead of warm liquid. He wraps his hand around my wrist and then guides my thumb over my abdomen, as if marking me with his scent.

I am wearing nothing and as my fingers caress his stav once more, I long to feel his hands on my body. "Touch me," I whisper.

I love that he touches my face first, running his thumb across my lower lip.

"You are beautiful, Alara," he murmurs before pressing his mouth to mine. "I desire you to be my mate."

"But I thought you said we could not—"

He places a finger to my lips. "Just tell me you will be mine and I will give you pleasure, Alara. We do not have to fully mate. Will you accept me, my Takara?"

"What is 'Takara?' "

"It is a word in the ancient tongue." He drops his forehead to mine and cups my cheek. "It means 'beloved treasure.' "

"Yes." I smile against his lips. "I accept you, Veron. You are mine and I am yours."

He pulls back to trail a line of kisses across my jaw and down my neck to my chest. He closes his mouth over my breast and laves the soft peak, turning it into a hard, beaded tip.

My pulse pounds between my thighs. I thread my fingers through his hair and arch into him, wanting more. He slides his hand down my body and cups my feminine place.

"Allow me to pleasure you," he whispers against my skin.

I nod and he dips one finger through my already slick folds, careful to retract his claws before he does so. I gasp as he brushes over the small bundle of nerves at the apex. Encouraged by my response, he gently teases the sensitive flesh and I grind my hips into his hand.

I've touched myself before, but it's never felt like this. Everything he does feels amazing. I want him to feel as wonderful as I do. I trace my hand down his body and wrap my fingers around his stav. He groans as I begin to lightly stroke his length.

He presses the tip of his finger into my core while he continues to tease his thumb over the sensitive pearl of flesh at the top. At first, the invasion is uncomfortable, but as he gently moves in and out, I relax, enjoying the way he feels inside me.

Liquid beads on the tip of his stav again and runs down his length. I gather the drop on my fingers, and he rumbles in arousal as I move them through my folds.

His breathing quickens as I wrap my hand around him again. More warm liquid covers my palm, and he grips my wrist, stopping me from stroking him.

"What's wrong?" I ask, worried that I've done something he does not like.

"If we do not stop now," he rasps. "I will claim you."

I hold him close. "I want you to claim me, Veron. I want to be yours in all ways."

Tenderly, he brushes his fingers across my cheek and then lies down beside me. He folds me up in his arms and wings and kisses me gently. "I will not risk hurting you, Alara. I am content to simply hold you like this."

I run my fingers through the hairs at the nape of his neck. "What if we just continue touching each other?"

"You like my touch?"

I smile. "Yes."

He slicks his fingers through my folds again and I gasp. I reach for his stav and begin stroking him as he teases my sensitive flesh. It isn't long before I'm breathless and panting beneath him.

Warm liquid drips from his stav as his arousal grows. I'm so close to the edge. I breathe in his ear, "Veron, please."

I do not even know what I'm asking for, but when he gently inserts one finger into my core, the small muscles of my channel flex and quiver around it. My entire body goes taut and then my release roars through me and I cry out his name.

He stiffens beside me. His stav pulses in my hand and then a hot stream of liquid erupts from the tip, covering my abdomen with his release. He splays his palm low over my belly and then rubs his essence down my skin to my folds, growling as he marks me with his scent. He skims the tip of his nose alongside mine and then kisses me long and deep.

"You are perfect, my Alara." His voice is a low rumbling purr.

"That was—there are no words," I breathe. I snuggle into him as he encircles me tightly with his arms and wings. I love the way his body feels curled protectively around mine. Reaching up, I play with the hair at the nape of his neck and bury my face in his chest. I inhale deeply of his masculine scent—a hint of fresh rain and forest.

"Your color is pink now," I tell him.

"Then that must be the color of joy." He combs his fingers through my hair and presses a soft kiss to my temple. "For I have never known such happiness before you, my Takara."

I trail my fingers across his chest and then rest my open palm directly over his heart. "You used to turn silver sometimes, a color I'd never sensed on anyone before. I no longer sense it as often and I wonder if—" I stop short, uncertain of how to explain.

"If what?" he presses.

I continue. "If it was the... Dragon part of you. The part that did not understand emotion."

He hums in the back of his throat. "Perhaps this is truth. I knew little of emotions before I met you."

I smile. My eyelids grow heavy as I struggle to stay awake. He gently kisses my forehead.

"I have something I have been meaning to give you."

Curious, I ask, "What is it?"

"I will return in a moment."

His footsteps retreat down the hall, but it is not long until I hear him return. The bed dips to one side as he crawls in beside me.

"Hold out your hand."

I do as he asks, and something that feels suspiciously like

a necklace is placed in my palm. I finger the delicate chain and feel the smooth, round pendant on the end. "What is this?"

"It is a blue pearl," he replies. "From the heart of the ocean. It is… my most valuable possession."

My mouth drifts open. "Veron, I—I can't accept this. It's too much."

He places his hand over mine. "I want you to have it, Alara." He rubs his cheek against my temple. "I want you to have the one thing that I used to value most above all others… before I met you."

Tears sting my eyes, but I blink them back. He pulls me into his arms. "You are my Takara—my most valuable treasure, Alara. I will never let you go. I will find a way to break the curse and free you."

Emotions lodge in my throat, but I somehow speak around them. "I love you, Veron." I hug him tightly. "Even if you cannot break the curse… you have made me happier than I have ever been, my love."

He pulls me to his chest and smooths his hand down my back. "I will find a way, Alara. My vow. Now rest, my human," he whispers. "I will hold you."

And he does, so tenderly my heart melts as I drift away into darkness.

CHAPTER 18

VERON

I lie awake as Alara sleeps in my arms. I am tired as well, but I do not wish to close my eyes. Our time together is limited, so I want to savor every second. I can hardly bear knowing that soon, she will die like the others—turned to stone.

I have pitied every female who suffered this fate before her, even when I barely knew them. Alara is the first one I have ever grown close to. The only one who has allowed me to touch her.

A smile plays across my lips as I brush back her hair from her face. Her long lashes fan over soft, pink cheeks. Her lips are open in a small O and her glossy hair spreads out beneath her like a beautiful halo. She sleeps so trustingly in my arms it nearly breaks me.

She calls me her Dragon.

My kind do not love. We claim and possess our mates, and the bonds we form are eternal.

But she has awakened emotions in me that I never knew

before. Deeper than the ocean and constant as the stars, my love for her is an absolute. It will not falter or fade with the passage of time and it will admit no other. She is mine and I am hers.

Sadness cuts at my heart. She is blind and will never look upon me as her true love. She cannot possibly break the curse. I will lose her.

As I look at her, I understand the depth of despair that the blood witch must have felt when I killed her mate. I wronged her. Deeply. And I realize that nothing I do will ever be enough to atone for this sin.

She cursed me for this. And I know that I would have done the same or worse if someone killed Alara. Now I understand for the first time exactly what kind of vengeance the witch wants to exact from me.

I push down my despair. Alara does not want me to grieve; she has insisted that we enjoy what little time we have with one another. This is what she has asked of me, and this is what I shall endeavor.

But I have not given up hope that I might persuade the witch to spare her. With a renewed sense of determination, I vow that I will do everything in my power to save my mate.

Quietly, I slip from the bed and stride to the balcony. I extend my claws and slice my palm to draw blood. Stretching my arm out over the water, I allow my blood to drip into the ocean below as I try once again to summon the witch. I have summoned her in this way in the past, and I pray it works now as it did then.

I walk back inside and crawl into the bed beside my mate. With my body protectively curled around Alara, I wrap my arm around her waist and tug her back against me. Gently, I nuzzle her hair and breathe deeply of her delicate scent. She is mine, and I will do whatever it takes to save her. Closing my eyes, I allow myself to drift away, dreaming of a future with my Takara.

* * *

A STRANGE NOISE startles me awake. My eyes scan the darkness, searching for any sign of an intruder. I flare my nostrils and detect an unfamiliar scent—a human male.

Heat flashes through me. Who would dare trespass here?

Carefully, I untangle myself from Alara and rise from the bed, slipping quietly down the hallway. I have no wish to turn this human to stone if he is merely lost, so I stay hidden in the shadows as I creep down the stairs, following the scent to its source. If this intruder means to harm us, I will have no qualms burning him to ash, but until I know his intent, I would rather be safe.

A man with golden hair stands just inside the entryway. A blindfold covers his eyes, telling me he has not stumbled into my castle by accident. He intended to seek me out, but why?

He places his hands along the wall, feeling his way inside. I note the long sword strapped to his back. Does he truly believe he would have a chance of defending himself if I chose to kill him?

Flames lick at the back of my throat as I step out of the shadows. "Why have you come here?" I snarl, the sound reverberating deep in my chest.

He freezes. "Are you the Dragon?"

"What if I am? Have you come to challenge me? Many have tried. All have failed."

"I've come for Alara."

Shock followed quickly by possessive anger rushes through my veins. I growl low in my throat. "She is mine."

"I—I know," he stutters hastily. "She took her sister's place. I am Garen, Lilly's fiancé. Lilly is gravely ill. She is dying and asked me to retrieve her sister so she could see Alara one last time. I came to beg this of you. Please, allow her to visit her sister."

Soft footsteps on the stairs behind me draw my attention. I turn to find Alara, covered in a night robe. "Garen? Why are you here?"

His shoulders sag in relief. "Alara, thank the gods you are well. Lilly is dying. She wants to see you one last time before she—"

His voice catches in his throat.

Alara rushes past me to embrace him. "Oh, Garen. What has happened?"

"She was so distraught when she found out you had taken her place. She cried for days on the hill, calling to the sky for the Dragon to bring you back. The healers believe that is how she caught a cold and fell ill."

Her eyes well with tears. "Lilly is dying?"

"Yes," he replies. "Her fever has not yet broken, and I do not know if it ever will."

She turns her head in my direction. "Veron?"

"Yes?"

She moves toward my voice. Reaching me, she takes my hand and gives me a pleading expression. "Please, I have to see my sister."

Her plea tears at my heart. I want to grant her this request more than anything, but it is dangerous. If she leaves the castle for more than a day, the curse will render me a mindless, destructive beast. A Dragon that will rain down ruin upon the village and the cities beyond. "You must return before the sun sets tomorrow."

Her delicate brow wrinkles. "Of course I will return, Veron. I would never abandon you."

Garen's head jerks back in disbelief, but he says nothing.

"Did you come on horseback?" I ask.

"Yes."

"How did you find this place? No one has come here in many years."

"I—I wasn't sure I would. I only knew that the rumors said you lived in an abandoned castle by the sea, beyond the forest."

My nostrils flare as I scent the air. "No one else came with you?"

"It's just me," he replies quickly.

I stroke Alara's cheek. "I will take you both back to the village. You will travel much faster this way. I will return for you at the edge of the forest before nightfall."

She stretches onto her toes and presses a tender kiss to my lips before resting her head on my chest. "Thank you, Veron. I will be waiting for you."

CHAPTER 19

ALARA

Veron takes us back to the boundary of the forest. The same place he first found me not long ago. It feels like so much has happened since then. Garen slides off his back while Veron wraps his tail around my waist and carefully lowers me to the ground.

I hold up my hands, and he gently places his snout against my palms. "I will be waiting for you, my Dragon," I whisper.

"Go," he says. "See to your sister. I will return for you before sunset."

I rub my hand along his jaw and drop a quick kiss on his cheek.

Then I hold out my hand for Garen to guide me into the village. It doesn't take long to reach our home. The familiar scent of lavender drifts in from the gardens, but beneath that aroma, I note a hint of sickness in the air. A smell close to sweat but with a bitter tinge. I recognize it well, for I tended many villagers who fell ill when the last plague came through. My heart plunges when I realize the scent must come from my sister.

I rush to the bedroom. I'm so familiar with our home, I don't even have to count my steps as I do in the castle. My entire being already knows this layout by heart. I kneel at her bedside and grope across the blanket for her hand.

Her skin is cool to the touch, and I wonder if this means her fever has already broken. My unspoken question is answered a moment later by the familiar voice of the town's healer. "Garen," he says. "Her fever is gone. She should recover soon."

Relief washes through me, so intense I could cry with joy.

"Lilly? It's me, Alara. I came back for you, my dear sister."

"Alara," she murmurs hoarsely and squeezes my hand. "I've been so worried. I feared you were dead."

I pat her hand. "No. The beast—the Dragon—he's not what we thought he was. He's a good man, as much a victim to the curse as we are."

"The Dragon let you leave?" the healer asks incredulously.

"Yes," I confirm.

Garen settles beside me. "Garen," Lilly whispers. "My love. Thank you for saving my sister."

"Saving me?" I ask.

"Yes," he replies. "I vowed I'd save you for her. And now I have."

"But I told Veron I'd be back before sunset," I turn toward him. "You heard me promise."

"You aren't going back to that monster. Not now when you are safe."

"He's not a monster!" I snap. "Veron is kind and gentle and—"

"He's a Dragon, Alara. You will die just like the others who have never returned if you go back there."

"It's not his fault, Garen. It's the curse," I explain.

I recognize the touch of Lilly's hand running through my hair. "You are safe now, Alara. Stay here. Garen and I will look after you."

"She cannot stay," the healer protests behind me. "She will bring the wrath and ruin of the Dragon's fire upon our village."

"That's nonsense," Garen growls. "She is staying here, and that's that."

The healer grumbles in response. "I will inform the mayor of her return, at least."

Without another word, his footsteps retreat toward the front of the house. The hinges on the door creak open and shut, telling me he has gone.

I squeeze my sister's hand again. "Lilly, I know you want me to stay, but I can't. It does not matter that I am home; my fate is already bound to the curse. It will claim me once the blood moon cycle ends. Please, try to understand. I have to go back." I pause. "I *want* to go back."

"Why would you want to return to the Dragon?"

"Because I love him," I admit.

She inhales sharply, as does Garen beside me.

"You love him?" she repeats dubiously.

"Yes. And I want to spend whatever time I have left… together." I know she will not understand, so I gesture to Garen. "You have Garen. I have never had a love of my own. Now that I have met Veron, I… I've never been so happy, Lilly. I don't care that our time is limited. I love him and I want to be with him for as long as I can."

Lilly and Garen are silent. I imagine they must be staring at me in shock. I fully expect her to argue, but instead, she replies, "I understand. I am glad that I got to see you once more, my dear sister. I wish—" Her voice catches. "I wish you were not bound to the curse. I don't want you to die, Alara."

I give her a warm smile. "Do not feel sorry for me, Lilly.

Love can turn any life into a beautiful treasure, no matter how short. I never thought I would fall in love, but now that I have, I wouldn't trade it for anything." I touch Garen's arm and then slide my fingers down his long sleeve to take his hand. Tears escape my lashes as I cling to them both. "I pray you two have a beautiful life together. I am sorry I cannot share it with you, but I am glad you have each other."

Lilly and Garen both wrap their arms around me, hugging me tightly as my sister sobs into my shoulder. "I will miss you every single day," she whispers.

"As will I," Garen murmurs. "You are like a sister to me as well, Alara."

"And you have always been family to us, Garen. Thank you."

An abrupt knock at the door startles us. Garen gets up to answer.

"What is the meaning of this?" His voice carries from the living room.

Lilly calls out. "Garen, who is it?"

Several pairs of booted steps sound in the hallway, growing louder as the people move toward us. Their auras swirl with angry red.

"Alara, why are you here?" I recognize the mayor's voice immediately. His normally blue color shifts between bright orange and red. "You are supposed to be with the Dragon."

I stand and face the doorway. "He will come for me tonight."

"Of course he will. You've angered him with your escape."

"Escape?" Garen interjects. "He let her go. He let both of us go when I told him that Lilly was ill and wished to see her sister."

"Your actions have endangered the entire village."

"No, they haven't," I snap. "I'm going back. The Dragon is

coming for me. I have to meet him at the edge of the forest before sunset."

"And so you will," the mayor promises darkly. "Take her."

Two sets of heavy boots move toward me. Large hands wrap tightly around my arms.

I try to jerk free. "What are you doing?"

"Leave her alone!" Garen shouts.

The sound of fighting and chaos erupts all around me. I don't know how many people have invaded the house, but the only voice that is familiar is the mayor's.

"Stop!" I cry and everyone goes still. "What will you do to me?"

I may as well ask because from what I can determine, Garen is heavily outnumbered and the last thing I want is for him to be injured—or worse.

"Only one sacrifice has ever run," the mayor says. "Many years ago, a woman escaped, and the Dragon brought devastation to our village and three more beyond it. We will not allow that to happen again."

"I already said I'm going back," I reply. "Let me go and I'll leave."

"Don't worry," the mayor assures me, his aura reddening. "We will take you back to the edge of the forest. We will not allow the past to repeat itself."

Thank goodness, he's finally making sense. They're taking me back to wait for Veron.

"Gather more bindings and wood," he commands, and I realize he is speaking to his men.

Bindings and wood? I open my mouth to ask, but my sister beats me to it. "What are you planning?"

"We're going to burn her as a sacrifice to the Dragon so that he will not take out his revenge on our village for harboring her."

Alarm bursts through me. "Wait! You don't have to do that! He's coming back for me!"

"He's the one who let her go in the first place," Garen cries.

"You expect me to believe the Dragon would just let her go?" the mayor retorts. "That's what the last woman who escaped him said too."

I still as I remember what Veron told me. If I'm gone longer than a day, he becomes a mindless beast, bent upon demolition and ruination. It has happened before. I remember the stories my parents told me of the day the Dragon blasted the villages with fire, enraged that one of his captives escaped. Now that I know Veron has a kind heart, I realize he must have tried to let her leave, unaware of how the curse would punish him.

The sound of Lilly crying rips at my heart. Garen hurls threats at the men who start to lead me from the bedroom.

"Wait!" I shout, and they halt abruptly. "At least let me tell my sister goodbye."

The mayor's color changes from red to gray, and I am comforted to know he feels at least a scrap of remorse for his actions. The hands release me, and I return to my sister's side.

I hold out my hand and her warm palm slips into mine. "Lilly, it's going to be all right," I tell her. "Veron will save me. I know he will."

"But you're still going to die." Her voice quavers. "I don't want you to go."

I swallow down the lump in my throat. "I love you, Lilly." Turning in the direction I last heard her fiancé, I call, "Garen?"

"Yes?"

"Please, take care of my sister. Promise me you'll both stay here, and you won't seek me out again."

"Alara," he pleads, sadness plain in his voice, "they're going to—"

I interrupt him. "Veron will save me. He'll come for me. I know he will." I take a shaky breath. "Promise me you'll both stay here. Take care of my sister, Garen. Live a long and beautiful life together."

"I promise," he replies as the three of us embrace for the last time.

Although it is difficult, I force myself to pull away from them and turn toward the door. "I'm ready," I tell the men waiting to take me.

A hand wraps around my forearm and yanks roughly.

"I will not fight you." My sister will remember this moment forever, so I speak as calmly as I can. I do not want her to know how scared I am.

Please, I send a silent prayer to the gods. *Let me be brave.*

The sound of my sister's sobs follows me outside. Angry red surrounds me as the mob follows us through the village. People shout various curses at me, incensed that I would risk their lives and homes by fleeing from the Dragon.

I make no attempt to defend myself—what could I say that they would believe? Tears sting my eyes and I struggle to blink them back. Even so, a few stray droplets roll down my cheeks.

When we reach a gentle upward slope in the land, I know we are nearing the edge of the forest. Rather than wait for me to climb on my own, my captors drag me up the hill by my arms.

This time, instead of tying me between the two poles, they lead me onto a platform. They move so quickly, I stumble on the last few steps. I would surely have tripped, if not for the large hand holding me upright, crushing my forearm in a bruising grip.

They bind my wrists together tightly in front of me. If

they believe I will struggle, they are wrong. I want Veron to rescue me. If not for my sister, I never would have left him in the first place.

Someone grasps my shoulders. He smells unpleasantly of earth and sweat, like he hasn't bathed in several days. He pushes me and I back away slowly until my back bumps into something solid. I'm about to ask what is happening when he lifts my arms over my head and tugs on my bindings to test that they are secure.

His hands fall away, and I hear him take a step back, probably assessing his handiwork. I pull against my bonds but realize I cannot move.

"What are you doing?" I demand. "Let me go! I won't try to escape! I'll willingly go with the Dragon when he comes."

Angry murmurs from the crowd below reach my ears. I wonder how many have gathered and why. Aren't they afraid of the Dragon? I'm glad my sister and Garen aren't here; I wouldn't want them to see me like this.

"All right," a man's voice calls. "It's ready. Pull!"

Without warning, my entire body is jerked off the ground. Panic floods my veins, and I kick my legs wildly, struggling against my bonds. "What is this? Let me down!"

The dark, heavy scent of pitch fills my nostrils, followed by smoke and flame. Fear skitters through my body as heat billows my dress around my legs.

"What are you doing?" I yelp in alarm.

"The Dragon will want revenge for your escape. We are offering you to him so that he will not burn down our village," the mayor answers. "Light the rest of it," he adds, and I realize he is speaking to one of his men.

A collective gasp rises from the crowd. The dull *whoosh* and roar as the tinder catches fire heightens my fear. Wood crackles beneath me while the heat intensifies. The soles of my boots grow warm. "Wait!" I cry desperately. "Please! Please, don't burn me!"

The horn blares behind me, signaling for the Dragon. I half-expect to hear the spectators running for their lives; no sensible person wants to be nearby when the beast emerges from the forest. But the mayor's voice silences the crowd. "We must wait for the Dragon."

"What about the blindfolds?" someone calls.

"We do not need them. He will not shift into his two-legged form. We only need him to see that we have exacted revenge on the sacrifice who escaped him. Once he gets what he is seeking, he should return to the castle and leave us in peace."

In the small part of my mind that isn't panicking, I wonder how stupid these people must be to believe his words. What makes them think burning me at the stake will satisfy the Dragon?

"How do you know?" another voice chimes in.

"Because the last time one escaped, he stopped the moment she died when he burned down her house. It is written in the village records."

The curse—she was tied to her fate as I am. Either her death was part of the curse, or Veron simply stopped by coincidence.

Fear overwhelms me as the fire beneath me grows hotter. "Veron!" I cry out, tears streaming down my face. "Veron!"

An ear-shattering roar splits the air. The crowd falls silent as the beating of wings sounds overhead. A great gust of wind swirls around me, followed by another enraged bellow.

CHAPTER 20

VERON

The blare of the Dragon horn echoes through the forest. I'm already halfway to the village and I do not understand why they would call me now. Something about the sound unsettles me. Furiously, I flap my wings and race toward the edge of the woods, almost afraid of what I will find.

Black smoke spirals up toward the sky near the village. The heavy scent of pitch fills my nostrils, mixed with the acrid scent of fear, so thick it almost overwhelms me.

When I reach the hill at the edge of the trees, my heart stops for a second, then begins hammering. Alara hangs from a cable overhead as fire blazes beneath her, the flames licking at her boots. Her face is a mask of unbridled fear as she struggles against her bindings.

"Veron!" she cries out. "Veron!"

Murderous rage explodes in my chest, and I release a bellowing roar as I circle overhead. "How dare you?" I boom, loud and deep. "You think to take she who is mine?"

"She escaped," a man calls. I recognize him; he was the witness standing nearby when I first took Alara. He straightens to feign confidence and strength, but his fear is evident in the ashen pallor of his skin and the tremble in his voice. "We offer you this sacrifice to appease your need for revenge."

"Veron!" Alara cries again. Her panic tears at my heart and I swoop down low, slashing at her bindings as I wrap my claws around her. Once she is free, I cradle her close to my chest, glaring at the crowd surrounding us.

"She must die!" a villager demands.

A volley of arrows flies toward me. They bounce harmlessly off my scales, but I worry they may hit Alara. How dare they endanger my mate.

I have seen and heard enough of their hatefulness. Drawing in a deep breath, I release a deadly stream of flame as I lift into the air, circling the crowd. Rage fills me as I rain down fire upon my enemies—those who would dare harm what is mine.

Terrified screams split the air. The humans scatter and race back toward the village.

I turn and give chase, following them as they rush to retreat. They will die. All of them will burn for trying to harm my mate. I let loose a thundering roar of anger.

"Veron!" Alara's voice calls out.

I glance down at her small form, safe in my talons. Her chest rises and falls rapidly, and her fear scent permeates the air. "Don't hurt them. My sister and Garen are in the village. Take me back to the castle."

Baring my teeth, I glance back at the village. Fire crackles in my throat with my desire to scorch the entire place to ash. But Alara is more important right now, and I need to return her to safety. "You are safe," I tell her. "We are going home."

She remains silent the entire journey back to the castle. Her silence fills me with worry. What if she is injured?

I shift midair as soon as we reach the gardens. Gripping her waist as I drop to the ground, I hold her securely in my arms so that she does not fall. Desperately, I brush the hair back from her face and stare down at her in concern. Tears stain her cheeks. "Are you all right? Are you hurt? What is wrong?"

She lifts her head. Her voice trembles. "I'm fine. I promise."

I rain a series of tender kisses all over her face, nose, and brow, so thankful she is alive and safe in my arms. Her delicate fingers brush over my face as I kiss away her tears. "I love you, Alara."

"I love you, too," she breathes. "I was so afraid. I don't want to—"

She stops abruptly and my heart clenches, for I know what she means to say. She does not want to die. Even though I was able to rescue her tonight, death is still coming for her. With each passing moment, it creeps closer.

As I stare down at her beautiful face, I can hardly stand the knowledge that she will be gone soon. I swallow against the sudden lump in my throat and press my lips to hers.

She is mine, and I will never let her go. Not even to the curse that threatens to claim her. I almost lost her today. Shuddering inwardly, thinking of what might have happened if I hadn't been close by when the horn sounded.

I will find a way to save her life, no matter what. No one, not even death, will take her from me.

"Oh, Alara," I breathe as I clutch her tightly to my chest. "I understand now what I stole from the witch—the one thing she valued most. I know why she cursed me as she did."

"What do you mean? I thought she caught you before you took her treasure."

Gently, I drop my forehead to hers and rub her back. I know now that in withholding the truth of the curse, I have been lying to she whom I cherish and adore above all else. She is my treasure and I have not treated her as such. I have touched her when I should not, asked her to be mine when she does not even know what I am and what I've done.

I must tell her the truth about the curse—the reason the blood witch wanted revenge. If I am to save her, she needs to understand my sins and the truth of what I am. My throat closes as I run my fingers through her long, satiny hair.

"What's wrong, Veron? Your color is changing between orange and gray. You are worried and sad in the same measure. Why, my love? What is it? Is it about the curse? Whatever it is, you can tell me."

I hesitate. How do I tell her my dark secrets? She believes I am good, but she is mistaken. She does not know the truth of who I am and what I've done. The only thing I care about is her. If she is going to be mine, she needs to understand my sins, and all the terrible things I am capable of. I take her hand in my own, squeezing it gently. "You have asked me before why the witch cursed me as she did, and I have never explained."

"You said it was because you tried to steal from her."

"It was more than that."

"What do you mean?"

"When I went to steal the witch's treasure, I—" I grind my teeth in frustration. I do not want to tell her.

She presses a soft kiss to my lips. "It's alright, Veron. Whatever it is, you can tell me, my love."

I draw in a deep breath and release it before I give her my truth. "I killed her mate and burned the city around her castle to ash when I tried to steal her treasure. I am the Dragon that rained down fire and destruction upon Bryndor."

Her mouth drops open. "Bryndor," she whispers the name in a voice so low I almost miss it. "*You* were the Dragon that destroyed it?"

I lower my head as guilt washes through me. "Yes."

Alara inhales sharply, covering her mouth with her hand. "No. That couldn't have been you."

"It was."

"How could you do it?" Her voice quavers and breaks on the last word. "Why, Veron? How could you do such a terrible thing?"

I hate the expression of disbelief and horror on her face. I know there is nothing I can say that could ever excuse my actions or absolve me of this sin.

"Tell me why, Veron! I need to understand."

Even though she cannot see me, I am unable to look at her as I give the only explanation I can, terrible as it may be. "I am a Dragon. When I flew over their city, the people of Bryndor shot at me with their pitiful arrows. It angered me that they dared try to stand in my way. No one comes between a Dragon and his treasure. I poured flames and destruction down upon them in my anger, not caring about the devastation I left behind." I pause. "But when I think of you, my Takara, I understand that what I did was wrong."

She places her palms to my chest and pushes me away. I allow my arms and wings to fall back to my sides as I relinquish my hold on her. "Alara?"

Tears stream down her face as a broken sob shudders through her. "All this time... I thought I knew who you were. But I was wrong. I thought you were the victim in all of this. But it wasn't you, it was them," she says accusingly. "The people of Bryndor and all the ones who have come to this castle since then. I know *exactly* why the witch cursed you, Veron. Why didn't you tell me the truth?"

"Please, forgive me, Alara. I was afraid to tell you. I did not want you to fear me… to hate me."

"I loved you. How could you lie to me?"

I reach for her, but she jerks away from my touch as if burned.

"No!" she snaps. "Leave me alone!"

Her words hit me like a physical blow. "If that is what you wish, I will go."

"It is."

A terrible ache centers deep in my chest as I stare across at her. I want so much to gather her in my arms and never let her go. But she does not want me, and she never will now that she knows what I have done.

Spreading my wings, I take to the air. I fly out over the sea and along the coastline, heading toward my cave. The haunting song of the merfolk drifts up from the ocean below as if taunting me. Would that Dragons were not immune to their siren call, for I would gladly offer myself to the sea to be rid of my pain and despair.

CHAPTER 21

ALARA

He leaves, and the world spins and falls from under me. I sink to the ground, clutching my chest as I gasp raggedly through hiccupping sobs. Tears spill from my eyes and stream down my face as I think about his words. Veron is not the victim of an unjust curse. He is the Dragon that destroyed an entire city—simply because he wanted the treasure in their castle.

He killed the blood witch's mate and I understand now why she cursed him.

I return to my room and curl on my side on the floor before the fireplace. The man I love is a monster, and everything between us was a lie. Unable to move, minutes pass like an eternity before I force myself to stand.

I move out onto the balcony and place my hands on the railing, recalling all the time I've spent out here with Veron. I reach up and feel the necklace he gave me. Clutching the stone to my chest, I lower my head and choke back another sob.

Despite what he has done, I cannot deny that I still love him. What he did was monstrous and unforgivable. But that was the past. That is not who he is now.

I think of all our time together. How tender and caring he is with me. He saved me when I was in danger. *Me*—a mere human that his kind normally care nothing about. He is not the same Dragon he was before.

He's different. He has changed and he understands now that what he did was wrong.

I reach up to wipe the moisture from my cheeks. I love Veron. And now I must find him and tell him this before it is too late. Before the blood moon cycle ends and I fade away into nothing. I do not want to go without him knowing that I still love him.

CHAPTER 22

ALARA

Grabbing the spare walking cane Veron made for me, I rush out of the castle and into the courtyard. I have to find him. He is not here, but I believe I know where he went. Now, I just need to find a way there.

I follow the sound of the ocean. Carefully, I tap my cane until I reach the edge of the cliffs. The dull roar of the sea drifts up from below, and I dare not get too close for fear of tumbling to my death. As I walk along the cliff wall, I realize that what I'm doing is dangerous. But I do not have a choice.

As I feel of my pearl pendant, beneath the neckline of my dress, I think of my Dragon. My time is limited, and I have to find him before I go. I cannot stand the thought of dying without telling him how much he means to me. I love Veron and I want to spend what little time I have left with him.

Although it feels like an eternity, I'm almost certain it has only been a few hours since I left the castle. Each time he took me to his cave, it did not seem very far, but flying is much different from walking.

A haunting melody drifts up from below, the sound so lovely it is almost ethereal. I remember hearing it before when I was with Veron, near his cave. It must be the merfolk.

"Hello?" I call out, hoping they will answer. Maybe they can help me find his cave, or at least reassure me that I'm going in the right direction.

The singing cuts off, and I stop, listening carefully. For a moment, the only noise is the crash of the waves below, and I wonder if they decided to leave.

"Come down to the ocean, dear human," a man's voice calls out.

"If you are one of the merfolk, I've no desire to be lured into the sea," I reply. "I simply need help finding my way."

"You do not feel a pull to the ocean?" he asks, a curious note in his tone.

"No. I am trying to find the Dragon's cave. Surely you know where it is, for I heard your song not long ago near that place."

"I will not help you find your death."

My brows lift. "Is that not the purpose of your siren call? Lure me to the water so that I may drown?"

"No," he denies vehemently. "Contrary to what you may have heard, the tales of our kind luring innocents to the sea only to drown them are not true."

"Then why do you do it?"

"Many want for a wife. Humans are rumored to be excellent lovers. Passionate creatures like ourselves. I have watched you with the Dragon. I want only to save you from him. Do you know who he truly is, my lady?"

A warm flush creeps up my neck to my cheeks at his forward way of talking. "Yes. He is the Dragon who burned the city of Bryndor."

"Then you understand why I wish to entice you from his claws."

"You misunderstand," I tell him. "He has changed. He is not the same Dragon as he was before. I… I love him."

A soft chuckle escapes him. "So that is why my friend's song did not have an effect on you. He had wondered about that."

"Please, I must find him before it is too late."

"Too late for what?" he asks.

"He is under a curse. I am bound to it as well. I will die at the end of the blood moon cycle and I must find him before then."

"So, it is true. There is a curse upon the Dragon and his castle," he says. "My people had heard of this but were uncertain."

This merman sounds friendly enough, but I'm not sure I can trust him. "What is your name?"

"Errik. What is yours?"

"Alara. Will you help me find the Dragon's cave, Errik?"

He is silent for a long moment. Eventually, he replies, "If that is what you truly wish."

"I do."

"You are close. Simply continue along the cliffs and I will stay nearby until you reach the cave."

I smile. "Thank you, Errik."

"Do not thank me," he replies somberly. "It goes against every instinct I have to help you find him."

His statement makes me curious. "Then why do you help me?"

"Because I heard him call the blood witch a few days ago. He offered his blood to the sea to try to find her, begging her to spare his beloved. I assume that since my song did not tempt you, he was referring to you, since you are obviously in love with him as well."

A smile crests my lips. Veron loves me. What more proof do I need that he is changed?

"Are you certain you wish to find him?" Errik asks.

"Yes."

"Have you heard of what happened in Solwyck?"

Recalling the story of Princess Halla and how she nearly died slaying the Dragon that burned their city, I nod.

"Then you know Dragons are dangerous creatures."

"I know, Errik. But Veron is different."

"I hope you are right," he replies. "You are nearly there."

A thought occurs to me. "You said you have been watching me with Veron. Why?"

"In truth, I came here to find him. I was told that the Dragon that lived in the Kingdom of Eryadon, near the sea, has something I need."

"What is it?" I ask, curious to know.

"I am uncertain. I was told that I would recognize it when I saw it. That it is powerful, and I would be drawn to it instinctively."

"What is it for?"

He hesitates. Finally, he says, "It is… for a friend."

I do not press him for anything further. The hesitation in his reply tells me that whatever it is, he is reluctant to speak of it.

He changes the subject rather quickly. The merman and I chat as I make my way to Veron's cave. I'm eager to find my Dragon again. I reach for my pearl pendant, pulling it free of my dress and clutching it tightly in my palm as I think of him.

When Errik finally tells me that I will find the cavern only a few paces to my right, I turn toward the ocean to thank him.

He gasps. "That necklace. Where did you get it?"

I close my hand around the pearl and clutch it to my chest. "Veron gave it to me."

"Please," he begs. "May I have it?"

My brow furrows. "I—" I hesitate, not wanting to give away my Dragon's gift.

"Please," Errik says. "I need it for Princess Halla."

I blink several times. "The Princess of Solwyck?"

"Yes."

While I do not wish to part with my necklace, I feel compelled to give it to Errik. After all, without him, I might have continued on past Veron's cave and never been the wiser.

"All right," I tell him as I begin to unfasten the clasp from my neck.

Warm hands on my shoulders stop me abruptly as the scent of fresh rain and forest fill the air. I turn. Moving my hands along his arms, I smile. "Veron?"

He wraps his arms around me, pulling me close. "What are you doing here? Why have you come?"

"I needed to find you. I—"

"Did you walk here all this way by yourself?" he asks, a hint of anger shifting into his tone.

"I did walk here," I state firmly. "But I—"

"It is dangerous," he growls low. "You promised me you would not leave the castle without me ever again."

"Don't you growl at me," I snap back, and he quickly stops. "How else was I supposed to get here? Besides," I gesture to the ocean, "I had help from Errik."

A deep growl rumbles in his chest. "A merman?" he grinds out. "You should not trust them. They are dangerous."

I place my hands on my hips. "Well, he said the same thing about Dragons. If not for him, I would have been lost. I probably would have missed your cave entirely, Veron."

"What are you doing with your necklace?"

"Errik said he needs it for Princess Halla of Solwyck."

"Why does the princess need this?" Veron thunders, and I realize he is addressing the merman.

"She made a deal with a blood witch and I am trying to free her from it," Errik calls out.

Veron grows silent.

I take his hand. "If it will help the princess, we should give it to him, Veron."

He lifts the necklace and pendant from my palm. "It is a… very valuable treasure. It is from the very heart of the sea itself. Powerful and—"

I shake my head softly as I rub my hand up and down his arm. "I don't need any treasures. All I need is you."

CHAPTER 23

VERON

My heart stutters and then stops in my chest. "You... still want me?"

She smiles. "More than anything."

"Treat her well, Dragon," Errik calls out. "Or you will know the wrath of the seas."

I growl again at the merman. He is lucky I do not fly down to the water and tear off his tail. Alara has no idea how dangerous merfolk can be. I grasp her forearm and pull her behind me, spreading my wings wide to shield her from his view. I see the way he looks at her. She is beautiful and if he thinks to take her from me, he is wrong. "She is mine," I grit through my teeth. "I would never harm my greatest treasure."

And yet, even as the words leave my mouth, I know they are not true. It is my fault Alara is cursed. And it will be my fault if she turns to stone because I cannot find a way to break it.

I take the necklace and throw it out to the ocean. "Take the necklace and leave us, you troublesome fish."

Errik leaps from the water to catch it. He holds it up before him and smiles as he studies it closely. "Thank you. I will tell the princess that you helped her."

"I doubt she'll want to know that a Dragon aided her," I mumble.

"I meant Alara. Not you." Errik laughs. "The princess has no love of Dragons, as you well know."

Crossing my arms, I scoff at him.

"Goodbye, Alara!" he calls out. "And thank you!"

"Goodbye, Errik!"

The merman swims away and when I turn, I find Alara flashing a dazzling smile at the sea. Acid bubbles up inside me that she would smile so beautifully for another. Fierce possessiveness fills me as I wrap my arms around her again.

Gently, I nuzzle along her jaw and temple. Flaring my nostrils, I inhale deeply of her delicate scent. "You truly still want me?"

"Yes. I love you, Veron."

Her words sound too good to be true and I struggle to hold back the hope deep inside me as I ask, "Even despite what I've done?"

"Yes, my love. You are not the same as you were then. You are a good man, Veron."

I drop my chin and give a long, low sigh. I do not want to push her away, but I must make certain she understands exactly what I am. "You love me as if I were a man, but I am not. I am a Dragon. And now that you know what I've done, you know what I am capable of. My people... there is a reason your kind call us monsters, Alara."

She shakes her head subtly as a tear slips down her cheek. My mouth is dry as I brace myself for her rejection. She stretches up on her toes and wraps her arms around my neck. Resting her forehead gently to mine, she softly kisses me. "You are not a monster, Veron. You are a Dragon. You are *my* Dragon and I love you."

"Alara," I breathe, unable to say anything more as my throat tightens. I cannot stop touching her as I kiss away her tears. "I love you," I whisper between each press of my lips to her petal-soft skin.

Lifting her into my arms, I carry her back to my cave. Carefully, I set her feet on the floor. I enfold her in my arms and wings and pull her closer to me, inhaling her soft scent deep into my lungs. I desire more than anything to claim her, but Alara is human and I do not want to hurt her.

Her warm hands skim over my chest and abdomen as she presses her mouth to mine in a tender kiss. "I love you, my Dragon," she whispers against my lips. "Make love to me, Veron. I want to be yours."

Her words stir the dark and primal instincts within me, dissolving my control as she runs her hands down my body. I cannot think beyond the need to bury myself deep inside her warmth and fill her with my essence, claiming her as my mate.

My stav grows and extends from my mating pouch as I bear her to the ground. I dip my hand beneath the hemline of her dress, tracing along the warm, smooth flesh of her outer thigh to explore the sensuous curve of her hip. A low moan escapes her parted lips and the last of my control crumbles around me.

When I reach the slip of material between her thighs, I fist the fabric in my hand. She gasps as I tear it from her body. I extend my claws and slice a line down the fabric of her dress, baring her lovely form to my gaze. I want nothing to separate her from me. My tail curls around her thigh, opening her legs, and I settle between them.

I know we should stop, but I cannot pull away. I've wanted this for so long, and my desire to claim her as my mate is overpowering. When she rolls her hips against mine, the delicious warmth of her center presses firmly against my hardened length, and it is the most exquisite torture I have ever known. I long to sheathe myself deep inside her.

I capture her mouth with my own. Curling my tongue around hers, I deepen our kiss. I wish to touch and taste every part of her body. I rip my mouth from hers and move lower. I tear away the fabric that binds her chest, revealing the pale, creamy mounds of her breasts.

I close my mouth over one soft globe. She moans as I stroke my tongue across the stiffened peak while I cup her other breast in my hand. Her entire body is so soft and giving. I long to bury myself in her warm, wet heat, filling her with my essence and claiming her as mine.

She makes another soft moan as I run my fingers through her folds, already slick with arousal. I brush my thumb over the tiny bud at the apex and she arches up against me as if demanding more.

Desire burns through me like fire. I long to possess her and to be possessed, to consume her and to be consumed, to join her body to mine and fill her with my seed so all will know I have claimed her.

Not wanting to hurt her, I struggle to maintain some semblance of control, but primal instincts surge through me and I succumb to dark desire. She is mine and I will wait no longer to claim my mate. I growl low in arousal. "I can scent your need, my beautiful Alara. Tell me you are mine."

"Veron," she breathes. "I'm yours."

CHAPTER 24

ALARA

He captures my mouth in a claiming kiss, stealing the breath from my lungs. He descends until his chest and abdomen press against mine while he balances most of his weight on his elbows beside me. His tail wraps around my thigh, opening me even more. The crown of his stav bumps lightly against my entrance.

He cups my cheek. "You are mine," he growls.

I shiver with desire as he slowly enters me. Tight heat blooms deep in my core as he breaks through my barrier, sheathing his length completely inside me. At first, it's uncomfortable just as I've heard it can be, but when he moves his hips against mine, I inhale sharply as the foreign sensation becomes more pleasure than pain.

"So tight," he rasps.

He groans as I wrap my legs around him. I run my hands down the length of his spine, feeling the flex of his muscles beneath my fingers as he begins to stroke into me.

I can feel every delicious ridge of his stav as he moves

inside my channel, making my entire body light up with pleasure. He covers my mouth with his own in a passionate kiss and wraps his wings tight around me, molding my body to his. He trails a series of kisses along my jaw and neck, creating a gentle suction against my skin that drives me mad.

Pleasure coils tight in my core. I run my hands through his hair, sighing a breathless moan as he shifts his hips and then sinks impossibly deeper inside me.

He clamps his hand around my hip, holding me in place as each stroke becomes longer and deeper. I cling firmly to him, loving the feel of his body over mine as I breathe in his masculine scent that fills the air around us.

He tightens his wings around me so there is no space between our bodies. His breath is warm in my ear as he groans my name. He captures my lips, curling his tongue around mine in a branding kiss as he pins me in place. Each thrust becomes stronger and more desperate than the last, as if he fears he will lose me.

The small muscles of my channel quiver and flex around his length as heat pools deep in my core. I gasp as he moves even faster, making each sensation that much more intense as he thrusts deep inside me.

He grips my chin firmly with one hand. "Tell me you are mine," he growls.

"Yours," I barely manage.

He drops his head to the curve of my neck and shoulder, grazing his sharp fangs across my sensitive skin. I thread my fingers through his hair, pulling him closer. I want him to mark me and claim me in the way of his people. I long to be his in all ways.

He sinks his teeth deep into my neck. Waves of pleasure ripple through my entire body and then I fall over the edge, climaxing harder than I ever have before.

His stav begins pulsing strongly in my channel. "Mine!"

he roars as his release erupts from his body, flooding me with delicious warmth that seems to go on forever. I hold tightly to him as he fills me with his seed, triggering another orgasm deep within me, this one more intense than the last.

His stav is still buried deep in my channel as he collapses on top of me. I love the press of his weight as his body covers mine. He growls low against my neck. "You are mine, Alara. My greatest treasure."

"And you're mine, Veron," I whisper as I brush my fingers across his lips. "My Dragon."

CHAPTER 25

VERON

After we make love for the third time, we lay tangled in each other's arms in my cave. I glance out the opening to the darkened sky. The stars shine brightly overhead as I stare at the waning moon. I wrap my arms and wings tighter around Alara, pulling her body even closer to mine.

I must break the curse. Because she is blind, she will never look upon me and see the man that she loves. Surely there must be another way. I have to save her.

Alara stirs softly against me. My stav extends from my mating pouch with the desire to join our bodies once more. But as the cool breeze carries up the cliffs from the ocean below, I worry she will be too cold if we remain here.

Carefully, I stand and pull her up into my arms. She rests her head so trustingly against my chest as I carry her back to the castle and up to our bedroom that it nearly breaks me. I must save her. The thought of her becoming stone is devastating. Not my beautiful Alara. She is my greatest treasure.

I lay her down in the bed beneath the covers and then crawl in beside her. Tugging her close, I gently skim the tip of my nose from her temple down to her jaw and the elegant curve of her neck. I love how strongly she smells of me after our mating.

I trace my hand down her body and cup her breast. Her entire form is soft and giving and I long to take her again. A soft moan escapes her as I close my mouth over her other breast, laving my tongue over the already stiff peak.

Her hands go to my head, threading her fingers through my hair as she breathes my name out like a sigh. "Veron."

Reaching down, I drag my finger through her silken folds. Her inner thighs are sticky and coated with my release. Something dark and primal unfurls from deep within me. I long to fill her again with my seed. Dragons mate for life. She is my mate, and I will never take another. I will find a way to save my beautiful Takara.

Alara's hand moves down my form, and when she reaches my stav, she inhales sharply as if surprised.

I give her a long and languid kiss. "My kind can mate many times before we tire or need rest." I brush a dampened lock of hair back from her face. "Open yourself to me, my beautiful Alara. I must have you again."

"Yes," she moans as I gently push her thighs apart and then settle between them.

I notch my stav to her entrance. I groan as I sink into her warm, wet heat and then growl low as I begin to stroke deep inside her. She is so tight, I clench my jaw, struggling to hold back my release. I refuse to climax before her.

It isn't long before the small muscles of her channel begin to spasm and clench around my length, clamping down so hard as she finds her release that it triggers my own. My stav pulses as I erupt deep inside her, filling her with my seed.

She cries out my name as she climaxes again. I roar as her

channel tightens around my length in rhythmic motion, as if trying to draw every last drop of my essence deep into her open womb.

* * *

WHEN MORNING COMES, I am reluctant to leave her arms. I tug her closer and bury my nose in her hair, inhaling deeply of her delicious scent.

She smiles up at me, gently tracing her fingers across my chest. "Good morning."

I slide my hand down her arm and entwine our fingers. "Good morning, my beautiful mate."

"Is that what I am?" She grins. "A Dragon's mate?"

"Yes." I cannot help the possessive growl that vibrates my chest. "You are mine, Alara, and I will do whatever I must to keep you by my side."

Her expression falls and moisture gathers at the corners of her eyes. "I am blind, Veron. There is no way I can break the curse, my love."

I place my fingers under her chin and tip her face up to mine. "I will seek out the blood witch. There must be a way. I will keep you safe. I swear it."

"How many days do we have left?" she asks softly.

My hands tremble as I remember the waning moon overhead last night after we made love. The new moon can be no more than five days away and the roses are already beginning to wilt. "A handful."

She runs her hand up my arm to my face and feathers her fingers across my cheek. "I want to spend my last days with *you*, Veron. Not searching for something that may not even exist. We have to accept that there may not be a way to break the curse, my love."

I jerk back from her touch, gaping at her. "How can you

say that? I must find the blood witch. It is the only way to save you, Alara."

She shakes her head slowly. "You don't know that." She skims her lips over mine. "Just stay here with me. We can make love every day until—"

She stops short as a tear slips down her cheek.

I brush it away with the pad of my thumb. "Alara, I want a life with you. I long for a future with you, my Takara."

A broken sob slips free. "It is a beautiful dream, my love, one I wish for desperately, but because I cannot see, I can never break the curse." She looks pained. "Please, Veron. Let's not speak of this anymore. Let us just enjoy the time we have left."

Anger burns through me. "How can you ask this of me? How can you expect me to simply give up?"

"You knew how this would end from the beginning. You were the one who told me what happens." She takes my hand. "I will fade away into nothing, but when I do, it will be with your name upon my lips, my love. My beautiful Dragon."

A strange mixture of sadness and rage fills me, so intense I can hardly contain it. I want to roar my anger to the stars, but I do not want to upset my mate. With a heavy sigh, I rake my hand through my hair, then glance out the window at the dawning sky. "I must check the forest."

"Why?"

"I want to make sure no townspeople followed us."

I doubt one would, but I want to be certain. After what the humans did to my mate, I will not risk anyone else sneaking into the castle like Garen did and trying to harm us. Besides, I need to get away for a moment so I can try to summon the blood witch again.

I don't care what Alara says, I cannot give up and I won't. I love her too much not to try.

I take her hand and lift it to my lips, dropping a soft kiss on her knuckles. "I will return shortly, my Takara."

She smiles and leans in to give me a hungry kiss full of promise. "Hurry back."

CHAPTER 26

ALARA

Veron leaves and I go to the cleansing room to bathe. My entire body is sore, especially between my thighs, but in a good way, reminding me I have been thoroughly claimed by my fierce Dragon mate.

I wrap myself up in a robe when I'm done and make my way down the stairs. I stop when I reach the bottom, listening for any indication that he has returned, but I hear nothing. "Veron?" I call out, just to be sure.

When I receive no answer, I start for the kitchen. However, as I pass the entrance to the west wing of the castle, my steps falter. I have wondered all these days what is down there. What does he hide from me?

I know I shouldn't, but I cannot help but be curious. Surely it will not hurt to explore just a bit while he is gone.

I place my hand along the wall to guide me, counting my steps as I traverse the long hallway. At the end, I find a huge set of ornately carved doors. My fingers drift over the scrolling vines and flowers that are carved into the wood.

Carefully, I push them open, the hinges creaking loudly as I step inside. My footsteps echo off the walls, indicating this space must be huge—perhaps a ballroom or banquet hall.

Something about this place unnerves me. It does not feel at all like the rest of the castle. There is a darkness here that I cannot explain, but can feel deep in my soul.

I begin counting again as I explore, wanting to make certain I can quickly escape if I hear Veron returning. A crisp, saline breeze permeates the air as the crashing of ocean waves sounds nearby. The warmth of the sun heats the entire left side of my body, telling me a row of windows must stretch along one wall.

I continuously sweep my hands in front of me to make sure I do not run into any furniture. Suddenly, my palms slap something hard.

I slide my fingers along the irregular surface and realize I've hit a statue—a strikingly lifelike carving. As I feel along the smooth stone, I marvel at the delicate features of the woman's face, with a fine jawline and cheekbones. Even her dress is expertly done, the stone perfectly mimicking the ruffles and pleats one might find in real fabric.

After I am done exploring the statue, I move further into the room and find another statue, as intricately carved as the first. I wonder who created such lifelike art and why Veron was determined to hide it from me.

I feel for the next one, running my hand up the arm to find its face. Carefully, I trace my hands over the woman's cheeks, brow, and nose.

My jaw drops and I feel light-headed as I recognize the familiar pattern beneath my fingers. This statue is a replica of my best friend, Mara. She was the sacrifice last year.

With trembling hands, I examine the entire statue. My heart hammers as terror tightens my chest. I am certain it is her. We grew up together and I know her as well as I know my own sister.

But how can this be?

Swallowing against the ache in my throat, I continue down a line of statues. Each figure is a unique woman. My breath comes in quick, shallow pants as I struggle to push down my fear. I cover my face with my hands as I realize the truth.

This is the terrible secret that my Dragon has been keeping from me.

The women don't just disappear like Veron said—they all turn to stone.

I think of Veron's words about how soon the blood moon cycle will end. Everything was different when I thought I'd simply fade away. But as my hands trace over yet another statue, this dark fate is one I can hardly bear.

A choking sob escapes me as the horrible truth settles in my stomach like a heavy stone. I want to get as far away from this nightmare as I can. I try to run, but trip over the foot of a statue and fall down. I scramble to my feet, but now I'm completely turned around. Panic sets in. I've lost count of my steps and my direction; I'm lost in a sea of statues.

Desperate to find my way out, I run my hands over the faces, trying to find the ones I've already felt to tell me where I am. But each one is different from the ones I touched before. Fear wraps tight around my spine. I'm lost and I cannot get out of here.

I open my mouth to call out for Veron, but the words die in my throat as I whimper.

A noise draws my attention, and I recognize the pattern and cadence of Veron's footsteps as he comes down the long hallway. I could try to hide, but I'm in too much shock to bother and I want only to escape this room. I don't care if he's angry that I'm here. I cannot bear to remain in this sea of frozen statues any longer.

His steps echo as he enters the large room. He stops abruptly and then rushes toward me. "What are you doing here?" His voice is thunderous.

Despite his anger, I'm so glad that he's found me. My throat feels thick, and I cannot speak. I cling tightly to him, burying my face in his chest. "Veron. Oh, Veron."

He wraps his wings around me, holding me close, as if afraid he will lose me like all the others.

Dragging in a deep breath, I force myself to speak. "Tell me the truth." My bottom lip quivers as despair and betrayal tear at my heart. "You said all the women before me just disappeared—faded away to nothing—but that was a lie, wasn't it? They are all here." I gesture around the room. "All of them turned to stone. Why didn't you tell me? Why did you lie?"

His color turns dark gray with sadness. "Because every female I told before you only feared her fate more. It was easier to let them believe they would simply fade into nothingness than to admit they would turn to stone."

I'm upset that he lied and want to be furious with him, but I cannot. I swallow against the constriction in my throat. "You were right. I wish I didn't know." My voice trembles and breaks on the last word.

Veron presses a series of urgent kisses to my face as he wraps his wings even closer around me. "Forgive me, my Takara. Forgive me," he pleads.

"Oh, Veron," I sob. "I'm trying to be brave, but I don't want to die. I don't want to be turned to stone."

He lifts me into his arms and carries me from the room and down the hallway.

"Where are you taking me?"

"To the gardens. There is something I must show you."

He walks a bit farther and then sets me down gently upon the gravel pathway. His hand takes mine, and he guides me forward until my fingers brush the soft petals of a flower. The bloom is beginning to wilt. "What is this? Why are you showing this to me?"

"When the blood witch cursed me, she left this rosebush behind. It synchronizes with the blood moon cycle. When the last petals have fallen from the blooms, that is when—" His voice catches.

He does not have to finish his sentence; I already understand what he means to say.

Fresh tears slip down my cheeks as I feel the wilted flowers. I do not have much time left. I jerk my hand back when one of the thorns pricks my finger.

"You're bleeding," Veron interjects. A warm drop of liquid rolls down my finger and drips from my skin. He rips a strip of fabric from my dress and ties it around the wound.

A whirl of leaves and petals whips around us, so strong it lifts my hair and the hem of my dress. A deafening crack of thunder sounds overhead. Veron wraps his wings around my body to shield me.

"Where did this storm come from?"

"I do not know. We should take refuge in the castle before it worsens."

We turn back on the path but freeze when a woman calls out behind us. "You summoned me, did you not?" Her voice is low and seductive.

Veron pulls me closer to him and snarls, "I have tried summoning you for days."

"Oh, I know," she laughs darkly. "But I thought I'd give you more time with your human."

A sudden rush of wind buffets us. Before I realize she has even approached us, she takes my hand. Her palm is soft and smooth, the skin of a woman who has never known a hard day of labor in her life. Warm air puffs against my neck and Veron growls a warning.

"So," she muses. "You have mated the Dragon. Does this mean that you love him?"

"Yes," I reply without hesitation. "I do."

She laughs, the sound light and airy, like wind chimes or bells. "What a shame you are blind and cannot look upon your true love, isn't it?"

"How, then, can we break the curse?" Veron demands, desperation lacing his tone. "There must be another way. Please, you have to spare her. I beg you."

She laughs again, louder this time. "My poor, sweet Dragon," she coos mockingly. "You have finally learned to love, haven't you? I knew that my test in the woods with the red Dragon meant you had finally learned. When I saw that you were willing to kill your own kind to save a mere human, I realized you had fallen in love."

"Please," he begs. "I understand now what I took from you. I know why you cursed me. Please, forgive me."

"Forgive you?" she asks. "No. I will not."

Two fingers tip up my chin, sharp claws pressing against my skin. I find myself curious what this blood witch might look like, though I dare not reach out to feel her face.

"It was your blood that summoned me," she says. "Tell me, what you would ask of a blood witch, my dear human girl?"

Veron wraps a protective wing around my side. "Be careful of what you say to her. She twists and bends words to do *her* bidding and not that of the summoner."

With Veron's words in mind, I think long and hard about my request. I must outwit her to get what I want, so I make my statement as plain as I can. "I want to be able to see Veron, so I may break the curse."

She snaps her fingers and the dark veil lifts from my eyes. I blink in shock at my surroundings, hardly believing that I can see again after so many years of blindness. I look up at Veron for the first time and reach up to cup his cheek, staring at him in wonder.

He is fierce and beautiful all at once. His silver scales gleam iridescently beneath the sun, lending him an ethereal glow. Layers of thick, corded muscle cover his body. His shoulders are broad, and his chest and abdomen are hard planes of chiseled perfection. I note the long slit of his mating pouch as my gaze travels down his form.

He is so handsome with a proud, square jaw that accentuates his aristocratic cheekbones, brow, and nose. Short-cropped, dark hair contrasts against his scales and short, black horns stick up on either side of his head above his temples.

Emerald-green, vertically slit pupils study me with such intense love and devotion, it melts my heart. He lifts his hand to stroke my cheek, careful to retract his claws as he touches my skin. "You are as beautiful as I imagined," I whisper.

His full lips curve up into a devastatingly handsome smile.

The witch clears her throat and when I turn to face her, I inhale sharply. She is the most captivating woman I have ever seen. Long, sleek hair falls around her shoulders in deep purple waves, only a few shades darker than her violet skin. Rich, amber, reptilian eyes narrow at me.

"Since you have not turned to stone, it seems you love him after all," she grumbles, not bothering to hide the disappointment in her voice. A sinister grin spreads across her face. "But this will work out even better than I'd planned."

Veron bares his fangs at her.

"What are you talking about?" I ask.

Her gaze shifts to Veron. "Arrogant Dragon. When you killed my mate, you took from me the only thing that mattered. Now, you will understand the pain you inflicted upon me as I take from you the one thing you treasure above all else."

He growls. "You cannot do this."

"I can and I will," she says darkly.

"Alara has passed your test. Lift the curse," he demands through gritted teeth. "Now."

She glares at him. "I will lift your curse, but not in the way you imagine."

Her gaze meets mine. "There are few beings more powerful than a Dragon. They care only for riches and treasure. Their hearts are hard and cold as stone. I had begun to believe it was not possible, but you—a fragile and pitiful human—have taught a Dragon how to love." She pauses. "When a Dragon takes a mate, it is an eternal bond. A Dragon's life is long, and he will have many years to mourn your loss."

"What will happen to her? Tell me," Veron demands.

She faces him. "Once the last petal falls from the rosebush and the new moon cycle begins, you will become as you once were—a Dragon. By your very nature, you will no longer understand or feel love."

"I would never forget my love for Alara," Veron denies. "Never. She is mine."

She purses her lips. "If that is true, then when the sun rises on that last day, if you look upon her and see your true love, she will not turn to stone."

An evil grin splits her face, lending her a sinister appearance that chills me to the bone. "But when you return to your true nature, dear Dragon, you will not love this poor human. I am certain. And if you do not remember that you love her, she will change into stone like all the others. Once that is done, I will return your memory, and you will live the rest of your life knowing that you failed her."

"Why would you do this?" Veron asks. "Why punish Alara for my sins?"

"Because," the witch levels an icy glare at him, "now that you understand love, I want you to suffer as I have since you killed my mate. I want you to live the rest of your miserable life knowing that the one thing you treasured most was taken from you by the one you took from first."

I hold Veron's hand tightly in mine as I touch his face, trying to offer him comfort. "It will be all right, Veron. I know it will."

The blood witch grasps my chin and gives me a pitying look. "No, it will not, my dear girl. You are cursed to love a Dragon, and Dragons do not love."

Veron bares his teeth.

"You should thank me, Dragon. Your curse has finally been broken."

Veron's hands curl into fists at his side. "How can you give me the ability to love and then take it away?"

"I did *not* give you the ability to love," she replies with a subtle smirk. "I only gave you a punishment... a trial so you could learn how to. Now that you have, you will understand my pain. You will suffer as I have ever since you killed my mate."

"Please," I drop to my knees before her. "I beg of you. If I die, do not give him back the memory of me. Please, do not do that to him. I don't want him to suffer."

"Oh, but *I* do," she replies as an evil grin curls her lips. "Dragons have long lives. He will have many years full of sorrow, pain, and regret as he grieves you for the rest of his existence. Only then will my revenge be complete."

"You cannot do this," he grits through his teeth.

"I can, and I already have. She wished to lift the curse and now it will be lifted. You are welcome."

With a mocking bow, she disappears.

Veron roars his rage to the sky.

I place my hands on either side of his face, drawing his attention back to me. "Veron. Stop, my love," I whisper. "Don't you see that this is a gift?"

He shakes his head. "How can you say this?"

I stretch onto my toes and rest my forehead against his as I stare deep into his emerald-green eyes. "My vision has returned. I am able to look upon you now, my love. And your curse is broken, my Dragon. You can live the rest of your life free of it."

"But when the sun rises on the last day, I will forget that I love you, Alara. I will forget just long enough to let you die. And then... I will remember everything after it is too late to save you. I'd rather die than lose you, my Takara."

I shake my head gently and press my finger to his lips to silence him. "*Shhh*, my love. Do not say that, and do not lament something we cannot change. Let us enjoy the time we have together, as you promised me in the beginning."

Reluctantly, he nods.

"Now, take me to bed, my love. I wish to stay in your arms all night."

CHAPTER 27

ALARA

He takes me to bed. His gaze holds mine, full of love and devotion, as he enters my body. With exquisite slowness, he strokes in and out, staring down at me as if memorizing the contours of my face.

He worries he will lose me.

I hold tightly to him as his thrusts become more urgent. His hot mouth descends on mine in a passion-filled kiss, telling me over and over again, "You are mine, my beautiful Alara. I will not forget you."

"And you are mine, my beautiful Dragon." I reach up and touch his cheek. "I love you so much, Veron."

We make love for hours. Each stroke becomes longer, deeper, and more forceful, as if he is desperate to prolong our time together. I cry out his name as I find my release. His stav pulses deep inside me as he fills me with his seed. He groans in my ear as he encircles me with his arms and wings, his stav still sheathed in my channel.

"I will not forget you, Alara." He runs his fingers through

my hair. "You are mine. More precious than any treasure in this world."

We spend the next few days wrapped up in each other. He hardly lets me out of his sight, as if he's afraid I'll somehow disappear.

As we lie in bed, he threads his fingers through mine. He lifts our joined hands, studying them intently before pressing a tender kiss to the space between my thumb and forefinger.

Even though I have regained my sight, I can still see the dark gray color of his mood. I reach up to cup his cheek. "I know you are sad, my love. I am too. But I want you to know something."

"What is it?"

I stare intently into his emerald-green eyes. "This month that we have had together has been the best of my life. Whatever happens, I will never regret this time with you, and I would not trade it for anything in the world."

His eyes brighten with tears, and he lowers his gaze. "Do not speak as if you will die, Alara."

"But, Veron, I—"

"I cannot bear it," he snaps. "Please, do not say such things."

He moves as if to stand from the bed, but I wrap my hand around his forearm, halting him. He turns back to me, and although he is a Dragon, it is easy to read the pain in his expression.

I open my mouth to speak, but he gathers me in his arms, crushing me to his chest. "How is it that my greatest sin is the reason I found you? I will make the blood witch pay if anything happens to you."

I push away from his chest and stare up at him. "If I die, I do not want you to seek revenge, Veron."

His brow furrows deeply. "Why not?"

"Because I don't want you to become like the witch—seeking revenge and losing your soul in the process."

He grimaces. "I am *nothing* like her."

"But you would become like her if you allowed the pursuit of revenge to consume you. And I don't want that for you, Veron. I want you to be happy." I meet his eyes evenly. "Promise me you will not seek revenge if I die."

"I want to crush her bones and burn her to ash," he grinds out. "I want to—"

"Promise me, Veron."

He huffs out a frustrated breath. "Fine," he grumbles.

Even as he says this, his hands are still curled into fists and he growls as he stares out the window. The angry red color of his mood tells me he's probably still thinking murderous thoughts about the witch.

"Stop growling." I tap his chest. "Right now."

His eyes snap toward me. He blinks several times and then shakes his head. He brushes some loose hair behind my ear as a smile tugs at his lips. "Only *you* would be brave enough to make demands of a Dragon."

I arch a teasing brow and then grin. "Why should I ever have reason to fear my Dragon when he loves me so?"

He lowers his chin to stare at me through heavyset brows as he moves over me. He lays me back on the bed, coiling his tail around my wrists and pulling my hands up to pin them to the pillow above my head. "You should fear me," he growls low in arousal. "Because when you speak to me so boldly, it makes me want to conquer you, my Takara, and never let you leave this bed."

"Conquer me?" I laugh softly. "You do not conquer me, my Dragon. You worship me, remember?"

A handsome smile curves his mouth as he leans in to press his lips to mine. "*That*, I do." He pulls back and his expression turns serious as he stares down at me. "I love you, Alara."

"I love you too, my Dragon."

* * *

AWARENESS SLOWLY TRICKLES BACK into my mind as I awaken. I open my eyes. The morning sunlight filters in through the window, casting the entire room in a soft orange glow. I glance out the window. The early rays of the sun peek over the ocean. It is the final morning of the curse.

Veron is out on the balcony, staring at the sea. I slip from the bed and walk to his side. He watches the waves with a faraway look.

I reach up and gently turn his face to me. "Veron?"

Instead of warm, green eyes full of love and devotion, I gasp as a stranger's eyes stare back at me. "Who are you?"

His words hit me like a physical blow. Devastated, I drop my hand back down to my side. "I am Alara. Your mate."

He narrows his eyes. "What kind of lie is this? You would dare try to trick a Dragon?"

Instantly, he shifts into his Dragon form.

I'm frozen in place as I gape at the creature before me. This is the first time I've seen him in this form. He's an enormous, towering Dragon covered in silver, iridescent scales. He is both terrifying and beautiful all at once. He flicks his long, tapered tail as if in agitation. His large, dark silver wings are folded tightly to his back.

Veron lowers his massive horned head. His large, green, vertically slit pupil contracts and then expands as it meets my stunned gaze. His nostrils flare, drawing in my scent before he releases a quick huff of air, nearly knocking me down.

"Veron?"

He tips his head to the side to regard me and then turns his gaze back out to the sea. He flexes his wings, spreading them wide as if preparing to take flight.

I panic. "Veron, wait! Do not leave!"

He turns back to me. "Why?" he asks, his voice cold and emotionless.

"Because you are my mate." I reach up and rest my palm lightly on his jaw. "And I am yours."

He regards me a moment longer, then glances back toward the ocean.

"Veron," I speak softly. "If you must go, know that I love you and I forgive you. No matter what happens, I will always love you, my Dragon."

He stills. Some hint of emotion flashes behind his eyes. "Your... Dragon." His voice is a low rumble.

"Yes." I nod.

A sharp pain stabs at my feet and I look down to see my skin beginning to solidify, gray stone traveling up my ankles.

"You are my Dragon, and I will always love you."

He stares down at me, his face set in a stoic mask. "Dragons do not love."

"That may be true of others, but not you." A tear escapes my lashes as I stare up at him. "You love me, Veron. I just need you to remember."

The hard stone continues up my body to my waist. It is not painful, but I'm terrified nonetheless. "Please, Veron. I am your mate. You gave me your mark... said I was your Takara—your greatest treasure. But in truth, you are mine, my love. You are my greatest treasure, my Dragon."

His gaze drops to my neck and the mark on my skin. A flicker of recognition flashes behind his eyes, sparking hope deep in my heart.

The curse continues up my chest to my neck, spreading to my arm that is extended to touch his face.

My voice quavers as I hold his gaze and stare deep into his emerald-green eyes. "Please, Veron. Remember who you are and come back to me, my love."

He closes his eyes and leans into my palm. "My Takara," he whispers. "I am your Dragon. You are my greatest treasure."

My tears fall freely, streaming down my face as my heart fills with joy. "Yes," I breathe. "I am yours and you are mine."

"I remember," he whispers, his gaze full of pain. "Tell me how to save you, my beautiful Alara. Please, do not leave me. I cannot live without you."

A tear slips down his cheek to my already encased hand, and I watch in wonder as the hard stone gradually retreats from my body. The gray stone cracks and crumbles away as I slowly regain my ability to move.

In a blinding whirlwind, he shifts forms and takes me in his arms as the last of it falls away. He runs his fingers through my hair as he stares down at me in awe.

"You are my Takara. You are my perfect, brave, and beautiful mate. The most precious treasure in all the world. You are mine."

"Yours," I agree as he leans in, capturing my mouth in a fiery kiss.

EPILOGUE

ALARA

The morning sun peeks in through the open window, casting a warm glow throughout the bedroom. Veron's arm tightens around my waist as he tugs me back into the solid warmth of his chest and nuzzles my hair. "Good morning, my beautiful mate," he whispers in my ear.

A gentle knock draws our attention as one of the staff speaks through the door. "The ambassador has sent word that he should be returning tomorrow, my lord and my lady."

"Inform me the moment he arrives," Veron replies.

"Yes, my lord."

I grin. When the curse broke, all the staff who used to run the castle reappeared. None of them remembered they'd even been gone. The same was true for all the women who had been turned to stone. I was thrilled to see my best friend, Mara, again.

Veron sent an ambassador to the Fae Kingdom a few weeks ago, and he has just returned. I hope he has good news, but I'm skeptical. The Fae consider Dragons their enemies.

Veron places two fingers up under my chin, tilting my face up to his. "Do not worry, my beautiful Takara. If the Fae will not help us, I will contact the Elves."

I arch a brow. "Don't the Elves hate Dragons as well?"

He narrows his eyes and growls. "I guarantee they will despise me even more when I rain down fire and ruin upon their kingdoms if they refuse to help us."

My jaw drops. "You cannot do that, Veron. You promised me you wouldn't—"

A deep rumbling laugh escapes him, and he drops a gentle kiss to my lips. "I will not destroy them, my Takara. But only because I promised you I would not."

I grin. "Thank you."

"But if they refuse to help us, we will travel to them and demand their aid."

I sigh heavily. "You must accept that it might not work."

He scoffs. "Of course it will work. You are not the first human who has bonded to an otherworldly being. I know for a fact that the Elves and the Fae have extended the lives of their human mates to match their own."

Veron wraps his arms and wings tightly around me as he strokes my cheek and meets my eyes evenly. "I will find a way to make them agree to help. After all," a faint grin tugs at his lips. "Who would want a Dragon as their enemy when he could become an ally instead?"

"You would become friends with your former enemies? Beings your kind have fought against for hundreds of years?"

He pulls me closer, and his green eyes shine down at me, full of love and devotion. "For you, I would do anything."

I wrap my arms around his form and press my lips to his. He rolls me beneath him, settling between my hips as he kisses a heated trail from my jaw down to the curve of my neck and shoulder.

I run my hands through his hair as he moves further down, then throw my head back and moan as he closes his mouth over my breast, lashing the peak with his tongue.

We make love three times before I manage to convince him that we should probably leave the bed sometime this morning—before the afternoon.

Snow falls gently outside the window as I snuggle against my mate. "I worry about my sister and Garen traveling in this weather to visit us."

Veron places a tender kiss on my temple. "If they are not averse to flying with a Dragon, I can retrieve them and bring them here from the village much faster."

I smile. "I know the villagers are more accepting of you now, but it might scare them to see you in Dragon form again, my love."

"Perhaps you are right." He moves his hand down my body and splays his palm over my lower abdomen. He leans in and licks the curve of my neck and shoulder.

"Your scent has changed," he says softly. "You carry my child in your womb."

I turn in his arms to face him. "You're certain?"

His mouth curves into a devastatingly handsome smile. "When has your Dragon ever been wrong, my Takara?"

A child. We've never even discussed children before because I did not think it was possible between us. Tears gather in the corner of my eyes as I place my hand atop his over my abdomen.

He cups my chin, lifting my gaze to his, worry evident in his features. "Why are you crying? Does this news upset you?"

A tear slips down my cheek as I smile. "I'm crying because I'm happy, Veron."

He captures my mouth in a fervent kiss and rolls me beneath him. His green eyes search mine. He reaches down to touch my face, staring at me like I am a rare and precious thing. "You are my greatest treasure, Alara. Tell me you are mine, my beautiful Takara."

He presses his lips to mine, and I smile against them. "I am yours and you are mine, my Dragon.

ALSO BY JESSICA GRAYSON

Next book in the series - *Captivated by the Fae: A Cinderella Retelling*

If you enjoyed this book please leave a review on Amazon and/or Goodreads.

Jessica Grayson

Fairy Tale Retellings (Once Upon a Fairy Tale Romance Series)

Taken by the Dragon: A Beauty and the Beast Retelling

Captivated by the Fae: A Cinderella Retelling

Rescued By The Merman: A Little Mermaid Retelling

Bound To The Elf Prince: A Snow White Retelling

Claimed By The Bear King: A Snow Queen Retelling

Protected By The Wolf Prince: A Red Riding Hood Retelling

Check out some of my other books while you're here.

Of Fate and Kings Series

Bound to the Dark Elf King

Claimed by the Dragon King

Taken by the Fae King

Stolen by the Wolf King

Captured by the Orc King

Of Gods and Fate (Greek God Romance Series)

Claimed By Hades

Bound to Ares

Orc Claimed Series

[Claimed by the Orc](#)

Of Dragons and Elves Series (Fantasy Romance)

[The Elf Knight](#)

Scarred Dragon Prince Series

[Shadow Guard: Dragon Shifter Romance](#)

To Love a Monster Book Series (Fantasy Romance)

[Claimed by the Monster: A Monster Romance](#)

Ice World Warrior Series (Scifi Romance)

[Claimed: Dragon Shifter Romance](#)

[Bound: Vampire Alien Romance](#)

[Rescued: Fae Alien Romance](#)

[Stolen: Werewolf Romance](#)

[Taken: Vampire Alien Romance](#)

[Fated: Dragon Shifter Romance](#)

[Protected: Dragon Shifter Romance](#)

[Chosen: Vampire Alien Romance](#)

Want Dragon Shifters? You can dive into their world with this completed Duology.

Mosauran Series (Dragon Shifter Alien Romance)

[**The Edge of it All**](#)

[**Shape of the Wind**](#)

V'loryn Series (Vampire Alien Romance)

[**Lost in the Deep End**](#)

[**Beneath a Different Sky**](#)

Under a Silver Moon

V'loryn Holiday Series (A Marek and Elizabeth Holiday novella takes place prior to their bonding)

The Thing We Choose

V'loryn Fated Ones (Vampire Alien Romance)

Where the Light Begins (Vanek's Story)

Settlers of the Outer Rim Series (Scifi Romance)

Rescued: Fox Shifter Romance

Protected: Lizard Man Romance

For information about upcoming releases Like me on

Facebook at Jessica Grayson

http://facebook.com/JessicaGraysonBooks.

OR

sign up for upcoming release alerts at my website:

Jessicagraysonauthor.com